I0689290

SUCKLE

A novel

by Benjamin Salmon

This is a work of fiction. Names, characters, businesses, places, events and incidents are either the products of the author's imagination or used in a fictitious manner. Any resemblance to actual persons, living or dead, or actual events is purely coincidental.

ISBN: 978-0-9978256-2-6

SUCKLE

March 26

Manuscript arrived today. Gave it a quick run-through. Rough but has a certain raw appeal. Amazing story, actually. Probably sell a million copies if the press likes it. Why wouldn't they? They liked it when it first broke, so why wouldn't they like it now? Remember reading about it in the Times myself a year ago. Had no idea then that I'd be working on the book.

Talked with John Fairfax on the phone to find out what he wants. Keep the voice intact, as much as possible. Lots of first-person inserts. Flesh out the back story. Add details. In a word: research.

Already set up appointment to meet with B. S. later this week. Flying out (coach) to Oregon for a couple months. I figure it'll be easier to work out there.

Gavin not at all impressed that I'm leaving during beach season on the Jersey shore. For the other side of the continent, no less, in cowboy country. Yeehaw! (Note to self: Is Oregon cowboy country?)

March 31

Checked into a hotel with a moose head over the front desk. My god! I thought Jersey was a forest. Dopey looking animal, the moose is. But the room is nice enough. Modern with just a twang of back country to it. At least there's a small desk-like piece of furniture in the corner of my room. Oh, and a well-stocked mini-bar. John F. will undoubtedly rue the day he agreed to let me work in backwater Oregon when he gets the tab from the Pinewood Lodge.

No cowboys, so far.

Went through B. S.'s manuscript again on the plane here. Marked it up this time. Lots of loose ends. Leads to follow up. I'm starting to wonder if I'll make it back to the Jersey shore at all this summer.

Who I Am and the Thing That Happened to Me

My name is Benjamin Salmon but people call me Benny mostly.
Not counting my wife Sam who called me Benjy when she was
trying real hard to get my attention. And I have to say
sometimes it could be real hard getting my attention if I
was busy with my trains or something but I guess it dont
matter much now shes gone anyway. Nobody calls me Benjy no
more. Mom called me Benjamin like it was supposed to make
me smarter or something but it didnt and I guess it dont
matter mostly neither now shes gone too. My dad called me
Ben till I was seven but he left after that so then he never
called me nothing at all. My stepbrother Ray called me
shit-for-brains mostly or whatever else that had shit in
it and my stepdad Jack pretty much never said nothing to
me cause I guess he was hoping Id just disappear or
something someday and I guess I pretty much did. But
thats another story or the back story like Mr. Fairfux at
the publishers says so I guess therell be more about that
later. A short introduction and get to the story he says
so I guess there it was and her it is.

My life was pretty much normal until a few months back.
Thats when this thing happened to me. Mr. Fairfux says
its something real special and I should write about it
cause its the heart of the story and Im pretty sure this
things not normal cause Mr. Fairfux wouldnt ask me to
write about it in the first place if it was something
normal. Anyway I never heard of it before and Phil never
heard of it neither. Phil is my brother-in-law and I
never told nobody about it but him. I mean I guess I told
Mr. Fairfux about it but it was after everyone else heard
about it too in the newspapers. But when it first happened
I just told Phil and I only told him cause he had this
thing with his testicles a few years back. Cancer I guess
it was. I dont know why it was real important to me but it
was. I guess I just thought he had some weird stuff going
on with his body too so maybe hed think mine wasnt so
weird. When I showed him he looked up at me from his plate
of soggy eggs shocked some and said You oughta take that
fuckin shit on the road Benny. But that was just Phil
always making jokes but mostly meaning nothing by it. It
was like part of his makeup or something or like the
grain of his wood I guess you could say. Phil works for
KNOB a local radio station with stupidly bad call letters.

Thats what Phil says and I guess I pretty much agree.
Phils not a disc jockey like he was before. Now he says hes
an on-air personality cause he dont spin tunes no more
but other people say hes just a shock jock like its something
bad or something. Phils one of them radio guys thats
always calling celebrities at home and telling them
theyre fat or saying some actor or hockey player is a fag
or calling some politician a douchebag. But Phil never
said nothing like that or not on the radio anyway. He cant
really call anyone a fag or a douchebag on the radio but
he might be able to call someone fat if its not a sponsor
or something and as long as they really are fat. Like I
said KNOB is a local station so it cant be real shocking so
I guess the real truth is Phil just tells kinda mean jokes
for a living and thats about it.

Not like me I watch people for a living. Im a security
guard. Its not my dream job or nothing but I could have
worse jobs and I guess Im mostly lucky I got the job back
at all after what happened. But I guess I shouldnt go
into that yet cause that comes at the end of the story.
Anyway Phil got me the security guard job after me and
Sam got an apartment together and got hitched right

after that. He said it wasnt right for a new husband to be
unemployed and I guess he was right especially cause we
had a little one on the way by then too. I mean I had a job
before that but I got fired or I guess they say let go now.
So like I said I got let go from my job. Before my security
guard job I work for West Coast Vending getting coins out
of vending machines. The day I got let go was like every
other day mostly until my last stop. I emptied them coins
into a canvas bag just like I was supposed to and put it on
the ground to close up the machine and I guess that was
my mistake cause I never saw the black dog coming. I guess
it was a Rottweiler or a Pitt bull or one of them other
mean kinda dogs. It ran by and all but knocked me down and
just like that the satchel was gone and the money too. I
chased that dog for a while but I guess it was in better
shape than me cause I couldnt keep up and after a while it
was mostly a small black dot on the road ahead so I gave
up and went back to the vending machine. Thats when I saw
it was emptied out and the keys were gone too. My boss at
West Coast Vending didnt believe my story and I got let go
that same day. You know how much fuckin work it is to
change the fuckin lock on every fuckin machine on your
fuckin route? He said to me. I said no cause the truth was

I didnt know how much work it was. Youre fuckin out of here he said. Get your fuckin stuff and get gone he said. I mean I guess I didnt really blame him mostly cause I dont think I woulda believed me neither if I was him and if it didnt really happen to me. But then a week later that dog did the same thing again to a bunch of other West Coast Vending guys like the exact same way it did to me. I guess it was trained like that or something. Anyway my boss said I could have my job back if I wanted but I said no cause Phil already got me a security guard job. No more vending machines for me I said.

———

So now I watch people mostly come and go all day downtown in the offices of Tower Plaza on a greasy security monitor and I have to say its not exciting like I thought it was gonna be. I mean security guard sounds kinda exciting and important too I guess like I might be guarding something valuable and stopping robberies or something but its nothing like that. Its pretty much the opposite of exciting. Boring I guess you could say. Not like Phils job. But there was some excitement a few months back when I caught a janitor putting his man-thing all over this chubby girls office stuff at night. I felt kinda bad cause he lost

his job after that but Phil said I did the right thing
cause the old perv was a real fuckin sicko and it was
primo shock jock material. I remember it real good cause
it was right about then this weird thing happened to me.
Its kinda hard to explain so Ill just come out and say it.
I started to lactate. I know thats what its called cause I
looked it up. Lactate: to secrete milk. Secrete: to produce.
But I guess I thought it was just mothers who lactate and
I guess I dont need to say Im not a mother. Im not even a
woman. When I said this to Phil he said No shit Benny. And
when he wanted to see me lactate right there I said Right
here? In **Big Boys**? And he said Yeah why not? Give me a
shot in my coffee. Ha ha I said but it wasnt a real laugh
but just the words ha ha. I told him its not like that. I
said I have to be kinda excited. Phil picked up his coffee
mug. What do you mean? Like Super Bowl excited? He stuck
his fat lips on the rim and slurped real loud. At first I
thought he was joking but then I saw he wasnt. He was
serious so I said excited like sexy kinda excited. Phils
Adams apple did this kinda tap dance thing under his
chin and I could tell he come near to spraying coffee all
over the booth. Jesus Benny! Is this some sick way of
tricking me into a homo thing with you? Has it really

been that long? So I pulled my fake Lacoste shirt tight against my man-boobs and I told him to watch. Then I thought about Rosie until it was like I could see the top of her head moving around down there or something and pretty soon a wet spot soaked the little green alligator with man-milk and thats when Phil said his thing about taking that fuckin shit on the road.

April 3

Met Benny for the first time today. We had lunch at Big Boy's. Yes, the same that he and Phil frequented back in the day (and yes there really is a big boy in front of it—creepy if you ask me!) Must admit to being curious about the author of the ms. Having read it through three times now. On the phone B. described himself as "short, bald, and dumpy mostly."He wasn't what you'd call short. Medium-height, more accurately. And not bald, but balding. The glossy, plastic-like skin stretched tautly across his skull retreated a few hard-fought paces back from the front lines of where a hairline had once barricaded itself against the inevitable march of time (not sure where I read that, but it's not mine—probably some dusty project from my past). In a word, B.'s hairline was receding. Only thing about his description that was accurate was his weight. Dumpy? Yeah, in that his stature was thick. Although he wasn't flabby. And not dumpy in the sense of disheveled. Far from it. He was neat. The sort who might press his underwear. But dumpy, as in overweight? Yeah, he was that.

If he were a woman, he'd be full-bodied. Maybe even Rubenesque. His breasts were full and round beneath a too-tight, knit golf shirt. Yes, his man-boobs were impressive. Tried not to stare but having just read his story (three times), it was a challenge to keep my gaze above his neckline.

He sprung up from the booth to say hello. Extended my hand in greeting but this only seemed to confuse him. Socially, a bit backwards, perhaps. No surprise, really. We sat and ordered food. Me a garden salad with an oil vinaigrette and he a bacon double cheeseburger with fries, chocolate-banana milkshake, and a side of tater tots and coleslaw. Eats when he's nervous, he said. So I asked him what he was nervous about. He was nervous about meeting me. When I asked him why he was nervous about meeting me he said because I knew everything about him. Not everything, I said, but I planned to learn a lot more if it was all right with him. He said it was OK.

I guess I should say Phil and I got along better after Sam died or better than when we were still brother-in-laws for real although I guess were still brother-in-laws for real even if the person who made us brother-in-laws is gone. But now I think about it Im not really sure about that just like Im not really sure why we got along better after Sam was gone neither. Maybe we needed something from each other like the way I saw on TV mooses and mountain goats need salt licks. I guess I should say Sam was my wife and Phils sister. She died having our little girl Becky. We already picked out the name and I guess Becky was Becky for about three minutes before she died too. That was three years ago and all that stuff they say about not a day goes by is pretty much true. Not a day goes by. My little Becky woulda been three years and three minutes old if shed lived and Id be bouncing her on my knee right now and Id be happy Im sure and Sam would be happy too. Anyway after Sam died Phil started coming around more. Hed just walk in and sit down without saying nothing and maybe hed watch TV for a while or maybe hed go out to the kitchen and do the dishes or go outside and water them dying rose bushes. Always something like that. Like I said we needed something from each other and I guess thats pretty much what Phil needed from me. He was going through a divorce around then so he didnt like to stay home much. His wife Steph pretty much moved out after the cancer made Phil into a kinda one-nut lunatic or something. Thats what Phil called himself mostly not Steph and not me but I thought it sometimes. The cancer never bothered Steph mostly and she probably woulda stuck around but Phil got all weird and sick and stuff and thats the real truth if you ask me. He kept asking people if they wanted to see his withered scrote or his one-melon gunnysack. When they didnt know what to say hed stick a hand into his fly and pull out a flap of skin looking like some shriveled up empty pouch or something. I wish I could say I never saw it myself but I did and it wasnt much to look at thats for sure. It was kinda like the pink and bumpy skin Sam used to pull off chicken breasts and throw into the sink but it wasnt really pink but it was more like black I guess. Anyway Phil come pretty near to getting himself fired from KNOB after that but somehow he didnt. He hung onto his job and then the shock jock thing opened up and it worked out pretty good for him Id say. It was real good for him to let go of all the stuff he was holding inside and I guess working for KNOB helped him do that some.

I took some time off after Sam died and I went through all the stuff that people go through mostly. I cried some and drank some but I never got weird and sick like Phil. Anyway six months later I was back at work bored and drinking coffee in front of the security monitor. I guess I was living like them people on them monitors I watched all day long. Gray and silent. For the next two years I lived gray and silent. A kinda pointless life is what Id probably call it now and I mean its a different kinda loneliness. Its like you know its never gonna go away and even if you do meet someone else thats nice even its still gonna be there like a kinda hum in the background or something that never goes away and you finally get used to it and pretty soon after that you even kinda like it. Kinda like the way I fall asleep watching TV I guess. Or at least thats how it seemed to me back then.

April 10

Tried to call Gavin tonight. Third time this week and still no answer. Wonder why he doesn't return my calls. Guess he's busy with Baby's Got Style. Sorry I won't be able to see his first Off-Broadway premiere. He's worked hard to get where he's at. But so have I. Knew he wasn't happy about me leaving, but I couldn't turn down this gig. It's not every day that you get a call from J.F. A special favor, no less. Could do wonders for my career. Might even lead to something permanent. How could Gavin not see that?

April 12

Wasn't hard to track down B.'s manager at West Coast Vending. A couple of phone calls and a quick car ride and I was sitting face-to-face with James Gomez, manager at West Coast Vending.

Interview Transcript: James Gomez

Me: Mr. Gomez, do you remember an employee named Benny Salmon?

JG: Yeah sure, I remember. How could I forget, him being in the newspapers and all?

Me: How would you describe Benny Salmon?

JG: Benny? Benny was a bit simple, you know? [winks] But he was a hard worker, and reliable too.

Me: What do you mean by simple, exactly?

JG: You know… not quite right in the head. I mean, he wasn't an idiot or anything like that. Just a bit slow, you know? I heard he got his umbilical cord wrapped around his neck when he was born. Not enough oxygen. Something like that.

Me: Do you remember where you heard that?

JG: Nah… that was just some rumor around here. I don't know who said or if was even true. But I could have been, you know?

Me: Do you remember why you let Benny go?

JG: I had to… I mean, I got people to report to, too, you know? The rottweiler thing was a fluke. Did it time and again after Benny. Just bad luck for Benny, I guess. I felt bad about it, you know? And I offered to take him back but Benny wasn't having none of it.

Me: Were you surprised when you read about Benny in the newspapers?

JG: Jesus's jukebox, yeah! I mean, Benny, our Benny, famous? All wrapped up in some cult thing and spraying milk all over cripples and what not. It was crazy, you know?

Then I Met Rosie (Who was also Norma but I Didnt Know it Yet)

After Sam died I wasnt thinking about meeting no one else.
It never crossed my mind but I guess thats when things
like that happen mostly when youre not thinking about
it. So thats when I met Norma but I didnt know she was
Norma yet cause she was still Rosie to me then. And now I
think about it I guess she was pretty much always Rosie
to me and Norma was someone I never knew from her life
before. Anyway I sometimes went for beers after work with
some guys from the Plaza. We crossed the street to this place
Orions Belt My Ass and I mostly just wanted beers to relax
and after some beers Id drive home to my empty place and
watch reruns of Barney Miller and fall asleep in front
of the TV like the way Jack always used to do. I remember
it was around Christmas Eve when I first saw Rosie in
Orions Belt My Ass cause the place was lit up with strings
of red and green Christmas bulbs like the real tiny kind.
It was packed mostly so we stood at the bar right in front
of a small mechanical Santa that farted the first line of
Jingle Bells when you tugged on his beard. One of the

guys Rudy cursed real loud and said I gotta get me one of
them. Him and the other guys from the Plaza were mostly
just looking for girls cause they said they were wanting
to stuff some Christmas goose and I guess its clear enough
what they meant by that. Rudy was the one that said the
thing about the Christmas goose but he was high on cleaning
products from work like he always was so I thought he
pretty much didnt have a chance of doing nothing but
getting drunk. Anyway like I said I was just there for a
couple of beers but when I went to the john there was this
girl in there getting sick in the sink. I mean the stuff
coming out of her was glowing like shed been drinking
them fancy radioactive kinda drinks or something so I
pulled out a bunch of paper towels and stood there waiting
for her to finish. She finally stood up and pulled her hair
back into a ball of frizz and there was a kinda shine on
her dark skin that was sweat mostly I guess so I handed
her the paper towels and she took them in her long nails
that looked kinda like bloody birds claws or something
and then she wiped her lips and face and she looked at me.
Im Rosie she said like she didnt just get sick in the mens
john. Benny I said. That was very sweet of you Benny. She
bent in and put her lips on my cheek and I could smell

some spicy kinda perfume mixed with tequila and vomit I
guess. Are you here alone Benny? she asked. So I said I was
with some guys from work. No I mean are you here with a
woman? Do you have a date? I didnt even know till right
then that she was a professional but I heard that line so
many times on TV I guessed she must be. No no date I said
and she sat on the sink and kinda opened her legs some. So
do you want a date Benny she said but before I could answer
Rudy walked in and blabbed something about flaming
Christians and I better get my ass back out there and get
sanctified. Rosie put a hand on my chest and she dug her
claws in some. Maybe later then Benny she said and she
kinda walked real unsteady and swayed some too out the
bathroom door. I didnt know you were into the whores said
Rudy. Black whores too. I thought I might knock him down
but I didnt. Im not I said and not cause she was black cause
I didnt mean it that way. I meant Im not into the whores
like the way Rudy said I was. Anyway I left Orions Belt
My Ass a while later and I was a little drunker than usual
cause I guess them Flaming Christian Christmas shots
pretty much did me in. My mouth tasted like candy mostly
and beer some but my legs were all rubber so I guess I
knew it was a good night for a taxi. I finally waved one

down and I was getting in when two hands reached around from behind me and I knew the bloody claws right away even though I was real drunk by now. Share a cab Benny? Said Rosie. I guess I didnt say nothing cause next thing I knew we were in the backseat and Rosie was doing these little kissing things on my neck kinda like a pigeon pecking at bread crumbs and I was sitting straight and stiff like I was a statue or something so she stopped pecking. Let me guess. You dont normally do this kinda thing right? She said. No I said. Married? she said. Was I said. Divorced? she said. Died I said. How long? she said. Three years I said. Oh Benny said Rosie and she sighed like she was sorry about Sam or like maybe she kinda died and disappeared from somebodys life before too. Then she dropped a leg over mine like if we were one person wed be sitting with crossed legs and she rested her head on my chest and it felt good. I mean I knew she was a professional and I was gonna have to pay money for it but it still felt good cause nobody touched me like that no more and I never touched no one else like that neither after Sam died if you dont count the bridesmaid at my bosses sons wedding two summers ago. She passed out on the sofa and I guess I kinda put her hand in my crotch but nothing

really happened and it wasnt much more than just a small
kinda scuffle between me and her boyfriend so I guess my
point is I didnt really care how much it was gonna cost
me. Anyway Rosie started doing the kissing thing on my
neck again and she slipped one of her claws inside my shirt
and started flipping my nipple up and down like the way
you flip a light switch with a burned out bulb on and off
or something and the whole time shes rubbing me with her
leg. At first I was thinking about the taxi driver watching
us in the mirror but Rosie didnt seem to care none so I tried
to ignore him too. She unbuttoned my shirt and starting
doing the pecking thing on my chest and she started licking
it with a real pink tongue and I mean I was getting worked up
by now and my man-thing was pretty much through the roof.
Next thing I knew Rosie was latched onto one of my man-boobs
and sucking like she was one of them baby deers you see on
TV they feed with them bottles. I mean she didnt call them
man-boobs but thats what Rudy and the guys and work always
said and sometimes they grabbed my man-boobs and squeezed
them like the way you squeeze a womans or something. Anyway
Rosie was sucking real hard and I guess what was kinda
strange was I really liked it. I mean it was like nothing I
ever felt before with Sam cause we were pretty normal having

sex and stuff and we never tried nothing like that.
Anyway just when I was feeling like I might shoot in my
shorts Rosie stopped all of a sudden like something was
wrong or like the way you stop chewing when youre eating
your Cheerios and you bite on something hard. I didnt
wanna say nothing cause I was breathing so heavy I knew
I would sound all shaky and out of breath if I did so I
just waited mostly even though my hips were still kinda
rabbitting up and done some. Rosie sat up and put a pinky to
her lips then she looked at the red claw and tasted it like
someone whos trying to figure out if the old mayonnaise
jar in the fridge went bad or not. Whats wrong? I asked. So
she pinched my man-boob and it squirted man-milk on the
plastic glass shield. Youre leaking she answered.

Before I go any further I guess I wanna say I never
cheated on Sam or nothing like that when we were married
and before she died and disappeared from my life. I never
went to the city looking for prostitutes or got hand-jobs
in Koreatown like Phil used to. I mean he never asked me
to go and he never told me about it or nothing but I knew
he did cause someone from work saw him there. I have to
say it was something I couldnt understand about Phil

cause he had someone like Steph at home. I guess I always had a thing for Steph but nothing never happened. Mostly nothing. One year we got drunk on Thanksgiving and when everyone else was passed out we kissed and I think I felt her up too but Im kinda foggy on that part. Anyway I know we stopped. I guess the truth was she stopped not me and we never said nothing about it and no one never found out. It was like it never happened mostly but sometimes I saw something in Stephs eyes and it wasnt guilt mostly. I guess it was more like she was ashamed or something but I couldnt tell if she was ashamed of what we did or if she was ashamed that she did it with me. And I guess the truth is maybe I woulda let it happen if she woulda and thats the real truth and the sad truth all rolled into one worse truth. I should probably say if you havent guessed by now Im not the handsomest guy in town. I mean unless you like fat bald guys then I might be handsome. But Im not real fat but a bit fat I guess and bald is pretty much just bald. I mean it dont matter how bald you are cause once your hair starts to go youre pretty much just bald to everyone else. Its kinda like you cant have half a head of hair the way you can be ten pounds overweight or something. Anyway Steph was a real pretty woman so for someone like me it was pretty tempting. So like I said maybe I woulda done it or probably I woulda done it I guess but I didnt and I guess thats my point mostly. And I dont wanna make it seem like Sam wasnt pretty or nothing like that. She sure wasnt ugly in no way but I mean you could say she was plain and that would be mostly true. But her kinda plain looked okay to me and parts of her were pretty good too. The one real good thing was her calves. They were something real nice to look at. I mean they were long and thin and muscley and I couldve watched Sam walk around in high heels all day long cause I loved the way her calves pulled tight and then let go. I only have one picture of them and it was at Sherm and Ellens backyard in front of their swimming pool and Sams in a swimming suit walking away from the camera. I guess I said something to her but I dont remember what cause shes looking over her shoulder kinda smiling like shes angry but shes not really and her calves are perfect.

Me and Rosie went to the Kings Head Hotel and rented one of them full suite rooms from an old guy that looked like he shaved with a sardine can lid or something. I mean his beard was all patchy and his face was pretty scraped up

and when he looked up from his paper he had that same
kinda dead man look on his face I remember Jack always
had when he came home from the picture frame factory.
Anyway the old guy seemed to know Rosie and I guess that
wasnt so strange cause I guessed this was where she came
to do business. The first thing I noticed when we got in
the room was a sawed-off broom leaning in the kitchen
corner and scratches on the inside of the door like maybe
someone used a gooseneck jimmy to break out or something.
There was a painting of a moon in a black lake above a
green sofa that sagged in the middle like it was a hundred
year old nag or something so I sat down on the bed and it
was pretty much the opposite of the sofa. Hard mostly
with just a bottom sheet and a thin blanket on top like one
of them kind that looks like its covered in tiny lint balls
or something but it isnt. Anyway I watched Rosie take off
her coat. Like I said before I was pretty much drunk but I
was real nervous too mostly. I mean I wasnt no real poon
pro in the sack like the way Rudy always used to say he
was. I never said nothing to him but I dont know how Rudy
could be no poon pro in the sack cause I doubted any woman
would get into the sack with him and even if they did he
was always high from sniffing floor wax so I doubted he

could do nothing in the sack except maybe melt or something. The truth was I pretty much figured Rudy for a self-service guy same as me. Rudy is younger than me by about five years and I guess hes single for good reason. I mean theres just no way around saying Rudys got himself a terrible complexion. Its like if he was a planet hed be one of them ones that was bombed by meteors real early on. Thats how bad it is. And hes always squinting and frowning like he ate a bad burrito for lunch or something. I guess the truth is no one at Tower Plaza really likes Rudy and no one wants much to do with him outside of work. The rest of the cleaning crew pretty much think Rudy is an A-number-one screw-up. An alcoholic screw-up and anyone will tell you thats the worst kind. I mean I knew he drank on the job for sure. When Rudy walked down the halls in his lazy way you could see the hip flask in his coveralls pocket swinging from side to side like it was a red flag or something. Anyway like I said I always figured Rudy for a self-service guy. When Sam was alive I didnt have to do much self-service except maybe when she was pregnant with Becky but after she died I pretty much started up again real serious. I guess I was about twelve when Ray first told me about self-service. I mean I knew he had a stack of magazines and he spent lots of time with them but I didnt know what he was doing with them mostly until he showed me one day. I told my friend Truck about it and he called me a fag and said he was tugging it for more than a year already. I wasnt sure why that made me a fag but I never said nothing to him about it. He said he had a secret to show me and so I followed him down to the swimming pool. When we got there I said this is your secret? But then he pulled me over to the change room windows and got on my shoulders and peeked into a crack. I guess it was the girls change room cause he started doing it right there on my shoulders. It was real uncomfortable and he was real heavy and kept moving around lots but then he shot all over the back of my head and down my neck and I was real mad at Truck for a while and he called me a fag when I didnt wanna do it again next time. Anyway one day mom caught me doing it in my room and she screamed like the way she screamed when she found our cat Poodles dead on the kitchen floor with worms coming out its mouth and rear. She made a real big deal about my self-service and she told Jack to talk to me and tell me it was a mortal sin and I better stop it or Ill go to hell but Jack just told Ray to go tell me instead. Ray came in and called me a

dumb shit and said do it in the bathroom like everyone
else and lock the door and I guess thats pretty much what
I did from then on. Anyway I guess my point is I did plenty
of self-service cause I wasnt real experienced with
women so I wasnt no poon pro in the sack like Rudy said
cause I only ever had sex with Sam mostly and the stuff we
did was pretty much normal. I dont know what I thought me
and Rosie might do but I guess I didnt think it was gonna
be normal like it was so I guess I was kinda shocked mostly.
I mean it was nothing like in the videos Ray used to watch
all the time and it was pretty fast mainly cause Rosie is
real sexy and I havent seen any naked women in person
besides Sam. Rosies black skin was so smooth and soft and
smelled kinda sweet even with the tequila and vomit and I
guess I pretty much shot before she really even got me
inside her. She said its okay like I did something wrong
and I said it was better than okay cause it was. Then she
laughed kinda breathy and surprised and said Youre
funny Benny and cute too. I guess I went all red cause she
did that laugh again and then she did that pecking thing
on my neck. Pretty soon she was sucking on one of my man-
boobs again and my whole body was tingling and I mean its
real hard to describe how I felt but I was all fuzzy like a

blurry picture or something or like there was an earthquake going on and I kept slipping outside myself. I guess it was kinda like that. Anyway Rosie stopped and kissed me hard at first and then softer and I could taste my man-milk on her lips and the truth is it wasnt bad mostly and I told her so. Then she said youre something very special Benny but I didnt really know what she meant.

April 24

Interview Transcript: Tony Walker

Me: I'm here with Cab driver Tony Walker. On the day that Benny Salmon first exhibited symptoms of galactorrhea, Mr. Walker was witness to the whole incident.

TW: What-a-rrhea?

Me: Galactorrhea… lactation… the flow of milk from the breast. Do you remember the night when a middle-aged man named Benny Salmon got into your cab and began to lactate?

TW: Is that what all this is about? I thought you were here about my demo tape. I'm a music man, a triple threat–composer, singer, producer.

Me: I did mention on the phone that this interview was concerning Benny Salmon.

TW: I thought Benny Salmon was a record exec at one of those new labels… Bad Apple or G-String-Strung-Up.

Me: No, as I said before, Benny Salmon is a middle-aged man who first began to lactate in your cab. Do you remember the night?

TW: Yeah, I remember. How could I forget? White dude with a black ho. Some kind of freak show in my back seat.

Me: Can you describe what happened that night?

TW: Can I? Yeah… like I said, a freak show. White dude is shitfaced… keeps saying something about flaming Christians and fartin' on Santa. The dude is seriously trashed, you understand. And the ho ain't much better… at least it seems that way. Sometimes they act all trashed out when they're not really trashed out, and then they roll you and leave you at the side of the road for dead. Not like that's ever happened to me, you understand, but I've heard about such things.

Me: Of course not. Continue.

TW: Anyway, she's on him like sweet, hot molasses… and the dude is groaning now… and I'm thinking he's about to blow his load in my cab… which don't bother me so long as his junk is still in his pants, which it was. But then the ho changes gears and starts fiddling with his titties. And the dude's got a rack on him, if you know what I mean. I ain't no turd burglar or nothing like that, but this dude has got some righteous knockers.

Me: Yes, I've seen them.

TW: Then you know what I'm talking about. Round and big and not too firm…

Me: I think we're getting a little sidetracked. What happened next?

TW: Well, next thing I know the dude springs a leak and starts shooting milk all over the Plexiglas. I'm trying to watch the road but at the same time I'm trying to catch a glimpse in the rearview mirror because I can't believe what's going on back there. I mean, the ho's milking the dude like Bessy the cow. So when they get out I tell the ho to clean that shit up, but she tells me to go fuck a fruit jar. Then she slams the door and they both stagger away. I never thought much about it till I saw a picture of the dude in the papers.

Me: And what did you think after you read about Benny in the newspaper?

TW: What did I think? I think that shit is fucked up. That's what I think.

How I First Found Sam (and Some About Truck Too)

Mr. Fairfux says I should write some more back-story about
Sam and me. I guess hes right cause hes the professional so
here seems like as good a place as any. Me and Sam met when I
was still working for West Coast Vending. One day I pulled
up to the vending machines outside Motel 6 and there she
was. Not like she was waiting for me or nothing like that
cause I didnt know her yet then. She was on the ground and
leaned against a coke machine in her underwear and not
real sexy underwear neither but the kind like when youre
a kid and you see your mom sitting at the kitchen table
having her first cigarette of the day. That kinda
underwear. I mean with real stretchy panties pulled up
to her belly button and a bra thats got steel girders in
it or something. Anyway I thought maybe she was dead at
first cause she wasnt moving and she didnt look real good
but there was no blood or nothing so then I thought maybe
she was sleeping or something. She kinda half screamed
and half snorted when I shook her and then she tried to
cover her woman-parts but I mean they were already
covered real good by her not sexy underwear. I tried to
give her my West Coast Vending jacket and I asked her if

she wanted to sit in the van but she didnt seem so sure
about that like maybe I was some kinda sicko like the old
perv janitor I talked about before but I was just trying
to be nice and I couldve done whatever she thought I was
gonna do to her before I woke her up if I wanted to. Like I
said I was just trying to be nice. Anyway pretty soon she
took the jacket and got in the van and I gave her a couple
of Twinkies and a Mountain Dew cause she looked kinda
pale. I didnt ask her what happened cause I didnt wanna
be pushy or nothing like that but I mean something
mustve happened or she wouldnt be leaning against my
coke machine in her not sexy underwear. Pretty soon she
told me the whole story and it came out of her like one
real big teardrop mostly like she just laid an egg right
there or something and that was the whole story. I guess a
teardrop and egg are two different things and Mr.
Fairfux will probably say I shouldnt mix them together
or something like that. Anyway I dont know which it was
for sure but her story was like one of them. She told me
her name was Samantha Wilkes and she was at the Motel 6
celebrating with some friends from college. I gave her a
Kleenex and she pushed tears and snot all over her cheeks
with it. She said she just got a nurse diploma and her and

the other nurse girls were out having some fun and they

played this game where they all got drunk and got naked

except she was the one who got drunk and naked mostly or

half-naked anyway. And thats when they sent her out to

buy cokes in her not sexy underwear. I guess the rest of

the story is pretty easy to figure out cause when she came

back the door was locked and the party just kept going on

inside without her. She said she still wasnt sure if they

did it on purpose or they forgot about her out there but I

could tell she was trying to convince herself they just

forgot cause she looked a little hurt when she said it. She

told me the music was loud and they probably didnt hear

her pounding on the door and this made me feel kinda bad

cause I knew people like them girls and I knew they didnt

forget about her. My stepbrother Ray was one of them kinda

people. He locked me out of our house in my underwear real

regular when I was a kid so I knew it was no accident that

Sam got locked out by them girls too. But when I pounded

on the door Ray came to the front window and laughed

mostly and pressed his bare bum against it until it was

flat. He called it making ass-pancakes and I guess he

thought it was real funny. When Sam and I got married

later Ray came to the wedding and I asked him about it and

he said he didnt remember nothing about making ass-
pancakes. I guess that kinda person dont think nothing
about locking someone outside in his underwear and I
guess that was the kinda people who locked Sam out of the
Motel 6 too. Anyway thats how I met my wife. My college
girl Sam.

May 6

Located one of the girls in Samantha Wilke's graduating class–a Christie Swanssen [with two "S"s, she quickly pointed out]. She didn't want to go on record [So why did she care about the two "S"s?]. Said she was at the graduation party at Motel 6 but didn't remember anything about Samantha being locked outside in her underwear. I asked if she remembered anyone going out for cokes from the coke machine. She said no. But everyone was drinking Jack and coke so someone probably had to go out for cokes. Said it could've happened that someone sent Samantha then locked her out because nobody liked Samantha much. When I asked why, said she didn't know. Said Samantha was a loner and maybe everyone mistook her shyness for an air or superiority (my words, not hers– she said "stuck up". Said she [Samantha] came from money, but no one cared because she never acted like it. Said if you come from money you "gotta act like it or no one's gonna give two shits." Asked if she'd heard that Samantha had died. Said no, and didn't seem to care one way or the other.

May 7

Finally got a call from Gavin. Wants me to fly into NYC for a weekend to see his show. I laughed, which he didn't like at all. How could I possibly leave now? I was just starting to piece together the bigger picture of B.'s life. Gavin didn't care. He needed me there.

G. is the assertive one in our relationship, the confident one, the driven one. But he's also the over-the-top sensitive one. And yes, sometimes the drama queen. He accuses me of being emotionless, unreachable. At times maybe I am. When you grow up in the closet you tend to be that–unreachable. It's a defense mechanism, and G. should know that. Although he's been out since he was old enough to wear his sister's training bra and wail out the chorus of "Cabaret" with warbling vibrato. Our different upbringings are like the shadows and light of Caravaggio's chiaroscuro when dragged into the intense light of honest scrutiny. Somehow they work together in the same way as shadows and light. Bringing us together in a meaningful whole, sometimes in rapturous glory. Sometimes not.

G. said he understood because he knew I was busy. He may've understood, but I doubted he accepted it. He slurped loudly from a drink (a black Russian, no doubt) before saying good bye and hanging up. Sat for a moment and wondered if he would ever call again.

Me and Sam started dating pretty much right after the coke machine thing. I mean I already saw her half naked so it seemed like a pretty good idea. I guess it wouldnt be real surprising if I said Id never been on many dates before that. Pretty much none in fact. I mean I went to a couple of church socials when I was a kid and there were girls there but I dont know if you can call that a date cause usually the boys were on one side of the table and the girls on the other. Me and my friend Truck would stuff our mouths real full with potato salad and say dumb French stuff like Ooh la la! and Mon cherry and an onion or radish or something would fall out of our mouths and the girls would giggle a real lot. Then Father Owens would come over and cuff us real hard and pretty much kick us out so we had most of the night to make trouble around town. Truck was my only friend when I was a kid I guess. He got the nickname Truck cause him and his Dad lived in an old Chevy two ton on the edge of town. I mean it was only a summer or so they lived in that old truck but it didnt matter cause after that everyone called him Truck all the time anyway. Before he was Truck his mom burned down the house and ran off with some city guy and

I guess Trucks dad was dead drunk and Truck pulled him
out of the fire and they sat in the Chevy and watched the
house burn down. For about three or four months I guess
they never really moved from the Chevy. It was like the
house was still burning or something and they were still
watching it so they just kept living there beside it like
it was a black skeleton or something from their life
before and they didnt wanna leave it behind. Anyway the
Chevy never ran so I guess you could call it a home. I
mean Truck did anyway. My mom always told me to stay
cleara Truck cause he was wild and even my stepbrother
Ray said so but I never listened to Ray much cause Ray
was mostly too stoned to say nothing smart about nothing.
And even after Truck and his dad moved out of the truck
into a real trailer my mom still said I should stay
cleara him. But like I said Truck was my only real friend
so there was nothing else I could do and he wasnt bad like
everyone said he was. I mean not so bad anyway. Sure he did
some stuff that was kinda bad I guess but nothing you
could say was real terrible bad. I guess the problem was I
was with him mostly when he did that kinda bad stuff and
after the blue paint thing we did to Mrs. Crumleys dog my
mom made me stop hanging around Truck for good.

I dont know why Truck hated Mrs. Crumley like that but he did. Mrs. Crumley was a hundred and two years old and that was the oldest person in our town. Maybe Truck hated her cause she was old and her being old rubbed him the wrong way or something. Maybe he thought hed be lucky to live half as long so it made him mad when he thought about it too much. I dont know. Anyway Mrs. Crumley was like a celebrity or something cause everyone treated her real special even though she was a mean old lady mostly. Thats the real truth and I guess thats pretty much what Truck thought too. Anyway Mrs. Crumley was real old but not as old as her dog Gus. Gus was one of them black wiener dogs and he was mean just like Mrs. Crumley too. Truck said Gus was twenty years old and that made him like a hundred and forty or something in human years and I mean I dont know if Gus was the oldest dog in town but he mustve been close. Anyway some TV people from the city wanted to come out and do a show on old Mrs. Crumley and her old dog Gus. It was one of them daytime shows I guess like the kind that interview people who write books about weird diet diets or making fruit wine from vegetables and sugar or mothers who are always getting depressed and take up knitting or something. Anyway the night before the TV people showed up at Mrs. Crumleys house me and Truck jumped the fence into her yard and spray painted old Guses coal hole blue. Truck held Gus real tight with both hands and I sprayed. I guess we woulda got caught if the old dog could bark some or had teeth at all cause Truck got bit a couple of times but he said it didnt hurt and watching Gus try to bark was kinda funny cause he was trying real hard but nothing came out like someone just turned off his volume or something. The show was on TV a week or so later I guess and Guss blue coal hole showed up clear as day when he was sitting there on old Mrs. Crumleys lap. Me and Truck never saw the show but we heard about it cause it seemed like everyone in town was talking about it. Ray said some kids in the high school started calling Gus Frank instead of Gus or Old Blue Eye but I didnt really know why they would or even why they thought it was funny. I guess most of the adults around town were pretty much ticked off about the whole thing with Gus and his blue coal hole and pretty soon the police found out it was me and Trucks doing. I guess Tom Barron ratted us out so Truck loosed the nuts on the front wheel of his bike and Truck got even when Toms

front wheel came off and knocked out a couple of his front
teeth on Logans Hill. I mean I didnt really agree with
that but I never said nothing to Truck and I thought I
should maybe say sorry to Tom but I never did. Anyway
when it was all over I got a couple of hard cuffs from mom
and a few kicks in the rear from Jack but that was about
it. Truck got it lots worse from his dad and he ended up in
the hospital for a couple days with a busted arm and a
couple of broke ribs. Like I said lots of people were ticked
off. Anyway me and Truck were never what youd call
popular but after that we were pretty much the most
unpopular boys in town so like I said before I guess its
not real surprising that I never went on a date with a
girl before I met my wife Sam. Sam wasnt real popular
neither and I guess the story about Motel 6 pretty much
proves that.

May 15

Interview Transcript: Thomas Barron

Me: I'm here at Dundee Central Bank with bank manager Thomas W. Barron. Thank you for agreeing to meet with me Mr. Barron.

TB: Call me Tom, please. [presents me with a business card]

Me: Tom, do you remember an incident from your youth with Gus the dog?

TB: Mrs. Crumley's dog, Gus? Yes, of course. Anyone who grew up in this area will recall the scandal surrounding Gus the dog.

Me: Can you tell me what happened?

TB: Well, as I think you already know, Benny Salmon and Truck Sloane spray painted the poor dog's rear end blue.

Me: And I understand it made it on to local TV. Is that correct?

TB: Yes, that's correct. Your Morning Joe with Josephine Sinatra.

Me: Sinatra? As in Ol' Blue Eyes? Wow! The plot thickens.

TB: Yes, Sinatra, as in Ol' Blue Eyes. Rumor had it that Josephine was a distant cousin of Frank, a rumor that she neither confirmed nor denied. I suspect it was started by her own people.

Me: Interesting. And is her program still on the air?

TB: No, no. She moved south to Hollywood shortly after to join the cast of some daytime drama. Apparently, when she got there, the producers wanted her to have some work done on her… you know [makes a gesture with two cupped hands]… breasts, so she did. But it turned out that the doctor's idea of a C cup and the producers' idea of a C cup were not at all the same. Apparently, the good doctor had done too much work for women in the pornography industry and his sense of size had become blown out of proportion, so to speak. In the end, Josephine's breasts were too large for daytime drama. So she ended up starring in adult movies instead.

Me: Wow! Tragedy or triumph? Not sure which. [shifting in my seat] Let's get back to the story of Gus the dog. What happened after the TV show aired?

TB: Well, as you can probably imagine, anyone with a conscience was outraged by the brevity–not to mention, the cruelty–of the act. It was scandalous.

Me: You keep calling it a scandal. Yes, it was a tasteless prank by two young boys, but does that really make it a scandal?

TB: Perhaps you don't know the full story. Gus died of rectal cancer not long after the spray painting incident. People around here blamed Benny and Truck for that.

Me: To be fair, the dog was exceptionally old. The spray paint likely had nothing to do with it.

TB: Not to the people around here. There was no question about it. Benny and Truck were responsible for Gus's demise. But the story doesn't end there, and this is where it becomes truly scandalous.

Me: Please go on.

TB: Old Mrs. Crumley was overcome by grief… so overcome in fact that she decided to try one of those dog cloning services.

Me: She had Gus the dog cloned?

TB: She did, yes. And that's when the trouble started.

Me: Trouble?

TB: You see, Gus the dog was a biter. Everyone knew it. He bit everyone, including Mrs. Crumley. But he had no teeth, so it was harmless and… rather comical, I guess, at times. But Gus the clone had a perfect set of teeth and he was genetically inclined to bite. One day, Gus the clone basically gave Old Mrs. Crumley a canine tracheotomy.

Me: You're not serious.

TB: I'm dead serious. She was asleep in her rocker when it happened. Investigators concluded that Gus the clone was whipped into some kind of killing frenzy by the clamor of Mrs. Crumley's prodigious snoring, which, it was later discovered, was the result of a severe case of untreated apnea.

Me: I'm at a loss for words.

TB: Now you understand why it is viewed by Dundeeans as a scandal… one that started with Benny and Truck.

Me: Truck accused you of turning him and Benny in. Did Truck attempt any act of revenge upon you?

TB: [Opens his mouth and points to his front teeth] Reconstructive surgery. I spent five years in a full-headgear brace because of him. Ruined my teen years. I can't say that I was sorry to hear what happened to him.

Me: So I have to ask, for the record: Did you turn Benny and Truck in to the police?

TB: Of course, I did! It was no news flash that they'd done it. I just confirmed what everyone already believed anyway.

—--

Sam got a job at a real big hospital in Seattle and I drove

out to see her on weekends in the West Coast Vending van

and we ate in the hospital cafeteria or ate a heated 7-

Eleven ham & cheese sandwich in the van. Nothing real

romantic. Not like them movies where you know everything

is gonna work out anyway so theres pretty much no point

in watching no more anyway. It wasnt like that but I mean

I liked her a real lot and she like me too so I guess it was

after about three months of me going back and forth that

we got a basement apartment together. It was kinda small

and one of them apartments where you see everyones feet

walking by your window when youre watching TV but it

was okay mostly I guess. Sam never complained about the

apartment much and she did stuff to make it nicer like

hanging pictures and curtains and putting on doorknobs

and she even bought a table for the kitchen so I could

throw out the card table I found at the side of the road. I

guess my favorite was the padded toilet seat and a clear

shower curtain with big red dots on it she bought for the

bathroom. Anyway it was right about that time that I

first met Sams folks. Sams dad Sherm owned a few hardware

stores around the county and so everyone treated him

real respectful. I guess I was pretty much nervous about
that but I was real crazy nervous when we pulled up in my
West Coast Vending van and I saw their big house and a
Cadillac parked in the driveway. Pretty soon though I
found out Sherm wasnt scary at all. He was real nice but
he looked kinda funny mostly cause his hands were real
big and his head was bald and real small and he talked
real loud pretty much all the time like the way a bus
driver tells the deaf old lady just sitting there that
its her stop. Even when Sherm was wanting someone to pass
the roast beef or the peas and carrots he talked real loud
and so I guess thats why I pretty much jumped out of my
skin when he asked me for the dinner rolls. Sams mom Ellen
scared me some just cause she wanted to know about my
family and I mean what was I supposed to tell her? My mom
drank mostly and I never knew my real dad very good and
my stepdad acted like I wasnt there and my stepbrother
smoked more pot than he sold and called me shithead and
shit-for-brains and shit-between-the-ears? I guess
thats what I shouldve told her but I didnt. I told her my
mom was in sales and my dad worked construction and she
smiled and made a sound like she knew what I was talking
about cause her mouth was pretty much busy chewing

roast beef. And I mean it wasnt a total lie but I guess it was partly a lie cause mom was a drunk waitress at the Thirsty Bear Saloon that was only working to pay off her bar tab there and Jack worked at the picture frame factory on the edge of town. I saw Jack there once stapling frames together that came down the belt and he looked pretty much like he already died or something and his life was his punishment. He just stared out at nothing mostly like anything was better than looking at what he was doing and I guess thats why he held the record for most trips to the emergency room. One year they pulled 48 staples from his hands so I guess thats why everyone at the factory called him Pin Cushion Kaczka. Anyway Ellen swallowed her roast beef and said and what does your brother do? Thats where things got real tricky cause Ray was doing three to five in the county lockup for dealing dope so I said he worked for the county and I guess she was just ready to ask more about Ray when Phil showed up at the house. Phil was still spinning tunes back then and he was still married to Steph. Like I said before Phil and I got along better after Sam was gone and I guess I mostly didnt like him much before that but I tried real hard to like him that night anyway. After dinner me and him went to the corner bar and all night he kept saying I better

not hurt his motherfuckin sister and I said I wouldnt

even though it was real hard not to laugh cause he kept

using his DJ voice like it would scare me or something.

Anyway we drank till the morning and then went to Big

Boys for the 18 Wheeler omelet with 18 eggs and I guess

that was pretty much the beginning of me and Phils

regular breakfast trips to Big Boys.

Me and Sam got married six months later at Country Lanes

Bowling cause the only public hall in town was being

used by the Mayor for a his granddaughters bat mitzvah

or something. I mean Sherm was respected around town but

even he couldnt outdo the mayor in importance so we mostly

had no choice but to find somewhere else. Phil suggested

the bowling alley and I thought it was okay since I spent

lots of time there anyway and Sherm said in his real loud

voice why not? Sam and Ellen made the place look real nice

even though it was a bowling alley and by that I mean there

was lots of white hearts and blue ribbons that matched my

blue tuxedo and Phils friend from KNOB played some rock

& roll records and there was free bowling for everyone

cause I mean that was the whole idea of having it there

anyway. Me and Sam won the couples bowling and I guess thats kinda right since it was our wedding and Sherm and Ellen seemed happy enough too cause Sherm kept telling Sam nice shot! in his real loud voice and Ellen kept taping up the decorations that got tore down by guests. So I guess things went pretty much as expected when I think about it now. I mean things went pretty much the way I expected anyway. Ray smoked himself into a daze and curled up on a bench and passed out and Mom drank herself senseless and then some and flashed her not-sexy underwear at the whole place over and over when she was bowling a perfect game of gutter balls and Phil broke Stephs big toe when he dropped a bowling ball on her foot. I guess he was drunk and holding two of them at his crotch like they were his testicles and one of them slipped and crushed Stephs big toe. It probably wouldnt have been so funny to him like it was if he knew a couple years later one of his real ones would get cut off and pretty much crush his own toe I guess you could say. I know theres a word for that kinda thing like the way something happening is like something thats gonna happen in the future too but Im not sure what it is. I mean theres a word for every kinda thing and its just a matter of if you know it or not so I plan to ask Mr. Fairfux about that word next time I see him. Anyway I guess the most surprising thing that happened at the wedding was me walking in on Jack having sex with Sams aunt Trudy in the mens bathroom. I mean he didnt really even stop or say nothing when he saw me looking at him in the mirror and Aunt Trudy had her head buried in the sink so I dont know if she even knew I was there. Jack looked mostly like he was moving something real heavy or something with his teeth gritted like the way they were. The truth is I pretty much never cared about what Jack did mostly and I knew he wasnt a good man or a good husband or nothing like that and him and mom never had what youd call a loving relationship but I guess I was a little surprised anyway. When I was a kid I cared lots more about him and I always wanted him to say something to me about anything but he never did. I guess I was like a stupid puppy Jack always kicked away and I just kept coming back for more.

June 2

Finally reached Sherman and Ellen Wilkes by phone. They refused to go on record with an interview. Had to pull some guerilla type shenanigans. Stopped by the Righty-Tighty Hardware store in Dundee, more or less cornered Sherman in his office. He was small, smaller than I'd imagined. A full head of gray hair that seemed not to adhere to any sense of order. A long crooked nose. White teeth–too white, leading me to believe they weren't his own. And curled slight shoulders that looked like they couldn't bear the weight of another misfortune.

There was so much to ask, I wasn't really sure where to start. So I started with Sam. Asked about her childhood. Sherman said it was normal, nothing out-of-the-ordinary. (His voice boomed just the way Benny'd described it.) Asked about Sam's teen years. He said the same. But this time wasn't convincing. Could tell he was hiding something. I tried to dig deeper. Was she unhappy? Depressed? Anything like that? He said something about no more than anyone else who's tortured by her peers. I tried to get more from him but he threw up a protective wall. (Decided to ask Benny more about that last comment later.)

Moved on to the topic of Benny. Asked him what he thought of Benny. Said he always liked Benny, even though Ellen never did. Said Benny was a bit simple, but he was a straight up kind of guy. And he made Sam happy. So what's not to like? Asked him why Ellen didn't like Benny. Said she thought he wasn't good enough. The usual thing that people with money say about people without it (his words, not mine).

We were interrupted by a phone call. A distributor of some sort had an appointment (Sherman opened a scheduler on his desk and plunked one of his big paws down on the page), so I was politely told to leave. I asked if he'd think about going on the record, let me interview him and Ellen. He said he think about it as he ushered me out the door.

Mr. Fairfux says I should try to convey my profound sense of loss when I tell the back-story and I have to say Im not real sure what he means by that cause I guess I never really thought about losing nothing before. Even Sam. I mean Im not a deep thinking man or nothing like that but to me people and things dont really get lost they mostly just disappear and I dont mean like in a magic trick or nothing like that. I mean like theyre just gone one day for no real reason that I can see and not really cause they got lost like the way I disappeared from mom and Jacks house when I was sixteen. I never got lost or nothing like that. I knew what I was doing mostly and that I probably wouldnt see them much if ever again. I guess I got the idea to disappear one night when I came home from making some trouble with Truck. Nothing terrible bad but a bit of trouble anyway. I was sixteen then and I wasnt going to school no more but I was looking for a job cause Jack said I should help pay for stuff around the house. Anyway when I came home mom was still working in the bar so she wasnt there but Jack was passed out in the front room like he always was and I remember I walked past him into the kitchen looking for something to eat and there was

nothing nowhere. So I went back out and sat down beside
Jack and thats when I noticed the bottle of pills in his
hand. The blue pills he was taking a real lot of lately
and Ray said they were for his nerves or something but I
never thought of Jack that way or nothing like that
cause he always seemed like he was somewhere else until
he suddenly snapped back to where he really was and
thats when he would explode like he was mad about being
woken up or something. Anyway that night sitting there
is his favorite chair he looked like a different kinda
dead than the dead I saw in the picture frame factory. I
guess this was more like the real kinda dead except he
wasnt dead. When I leaned in close I could hear him
breathing real slow and weak but I wasnt sure if he would
keep breathing like that or not. I dont really know why
but I decided then I was gonna leave and not come back.
Maybe I didnt wanna be around if Jack was really gonna
be dead. I thought about it a few times after that and I
still dont know why for sure. So anyway I called 9-1-1 and
told them Jack might be dying or something and then I
left for good. I disappeared from Jacks life like the way
he always wanted me too but it mightve been too late cause
Jack mostly looked like he was gonna disappear for good

from his own life first. Theres a word for that too I think and Ill ask Mr. Fairfux about it later. Anyway Jack didnt disappear for good from his own life but he couldve and I guess thats my point. Anyone can disappear at pretty much anytime.

May 22

Found Jack Kaczka in an extended care facility in Eugene. Looked like he was on his last legs, figuratively speaking, that is. His legs-legs were fine. He was one of the few patients who didn't need a wheelchair to get around. It was Jack's hands that were afflicted by tetanus it turned out. The many staples he'd sunk into his hands (either accidently or purposefully–it wasn't clear which) had taken their toll on him. His hands, two gnarled claws that he kept tucked inside the pockets of his threadbare terrycloth housecoat. The pleasingly angled features of his one-time matinee-idol good looks were apparent even in this condition (and even at his age), perhaps a little rounder is all. That Benny's mom, Beatrice Salmon, nee Schnell, once found Jack Kaczka so attractive came as no surprise. (In my circle of friends we would call him a dinky-boy doll.)

Along with Jack's physical affliction, Alzheimer's had set in. Didn't know how much I'd be able to extract from him in an interview. But figured I had to give it a try.

Interview Transcript: Jack Kaczka

Me: Thanks for seeing me Mr. Kaczka. I'd like to ask you about your time with Beatrice Salmon.

JK: Bea? She's dead. Drunk herself into a grave, just like I always said she would.

Me: Yes, I'm aware that she's passed on. As I said earlier, I'm helping Benny to write a book and I'm trying to fill in some of the details.

JK: Benny? That pot-smoking little shit? Always getting high up in the garage.

Me: No, actually, I think you're confusing Benny with Raymond– you're son Raymond. He spent some time in the state penitentiary for the distribution of marijuana.

JK: Raymond? Who the fuck is Raymond?

Me: Ray…

JK: Oh that good-for-nothing… yeah, he's mine. He was a pothead, too. Just like Benny.

Me: I wasn't aware that Benny smoked marijuana.

JK: Ha! Course he did. Him and that ne'er-do-well buddy of his were always high on something… what was that kid's name… "Trigger"?

Me: Truck.

JK: Yeah, Truck. I mean, who the hell name's his kid Trigger?

Me: You mean, Truck.

JK: What did I say?

Me: Never mind that. It's my understanding that "Truck"was just a nickname.

JK: Nickname? Whatever happened to "Teddy"and "Hal"? Those were nicknames.

Me: Let's get back to Ray. Was he you're only child?

JK: I sure-as-shit hope so. One a that boy was too many.

Me: Ray was from a former marriage?

JK: Never married. His ma disappeared one day and left him with me. Joined some band that was supposed be better than the Mommas and Pappas and moved to San Francisco. Good riddance, I said.

Me: Was she living with you at the time?

JK: Half the time. The other half, I don't know where she was. Probably out giving it to the Pappas, if you know what I mean.

Me: Ah… I think I do, yes. So after Ray's mother disappeared, you met Bea. Is that right?

JK: Uh-huh. She was a nurse or some such thing at the time.

Me: I don't think she was ever a nurse. But she was a waitress in the Thirsty Bear Saloon. Does that ring a bell?

JK: Thirsty Bear… yeah, rings a bell. Bea was a waitress there. That's right.

Me: So you remember that you met her there and moved in with her sometime after Ray's mother left for San Francisco.

JK: I remember. We had a connection–her old man hit the road, too. Left her and that dipshit Benny for good. He was… [raises one of his claws and makes an undecipherable gesture with it]… you know.

Me: No, I'm sorry. I didn't get that. He was what?

JK: You know… he liked… men [said with painful pleasure].

Me: Oh, Martin Salmon was gay?

JK: [wags his head] Gayer than Gatsby's flapper.

Me: I thought he left to live like a black bear in the woods of Canada… and that he may have been running from the law.

JK: Who told you that?

Me: Well, Benny, wrote that in his book.

JK: [laughs/hacks loudly] That dipshit wrote a book? He couldn't even spell his own name let alone write a book.

Me: I assure you… he did write a book and he can spell his own name. But that's beside the point. Let's get back to Martin being gay. So, Martin left because he was gay?

JK: Everyone in town knew it. The whole tough-guy garage thing was just a cover. If you ever saw him in his tight coveralls with his hair slicked back… you'd know he was gayer than shit.

Me: So why did he leave?

JK: Rumor around town was he had some Italian pufta up in Vancouver. That's where he went.

Me: You're sure about that?

JK: Oh, he was a fudge packer, all right. You only had to take one look at him to know it. Like I said, the Italian pufta was rumor. But I tell you one thing–Martin Salmon wouldn't last a day in the Rockies of Canada. Unless maybe he ran across a black bear who liked taking it up the stove pipe.

Me: Let's move on to something else. Do you remember the day Benny left?

JK: Left? He never left. He was like a wolf or some damn thing, circling the perimeter, sneaking in and taking whatever he needed whenever he needed it. I think he was living in them woods behind Flanagan's field for a while. But you could always tell when Benny had been around 'cause something was missing. A wrench, a magazine, a carton of milk or a can of tuna. Something.

Me: Were you happy that he wasn't really around much, then?

JK: Me? Coulda cared less. I never paid him no mind anyhow. Although his momma was plenty upset. She cried for damn days. And drank, too, of course. I think that dipshit Benny may've taken ten years off his momma's life when he left.

Me: Do you know what happened to Benny last year? Did you see it in the papers?

JK: [Looking confused] Benny? Who the hell is Benny? [Looking more confused] Are you that new doctor that's supposed to be coming round to see me? My prostate's killing me, doc.

Some Things That Happened Next (and Maybe Some More Back-Story)

Me and Sam moved from the basement apartment into a house pretty much right after we got married. I mean it wasnt nothing special and nothing like Sherm and Ellens place but it had a yard and a driveway and some flower beds and some stairs going up and down and a basement for my trains and the kitchen and front room were separated by a wall so Sam didnt complain about being able to hear me peeing in the toilet when she was cooking or watching TV like she could at the old place. I wasnt working for West Coast Vending no more so I didnt have no money but Sam got promoted at the hospital so I guess we could afford the place mostly. Like I said it wasnt nothing great but it was pretty much a palace to us after the basement apartment so we put up a few things together like pictures and curtains and bought a couple of lamps and a welcome mat without fighting mostly cause I went along with whatever Sam liked. I mean pink or purple or yellow dont matter none to me. Not like Phil and Steph. They couldnt buy nothing without fighting and the bad part about that was me and Sam was the ones they always called to come over and settle things when they had a fight. Sometimes it got pretty bad I mean like stupid bad or even painful bad. Like the time they called and Steph was screaming in the phone and Phil was screaming in the background and now that I think about it it was mostly like every other time too. Anyway we drove over to their house to make sure things were okay. I got to the kitchen and Phil was lying there on the floor moaning cause his hair was all tangled in the beaters of a hand mixer. I should probably say Phil was still a DJ then so I guess he thought he needed long hair. Anyway his hair was wrapped real tight in the beaters and I couldnt get it out so I unplugged the mixer and walked him over to a chair and Phil was holding onto the mixer so it wouldnt pull out his hair. I figured there was nothing else to do but cut his hair off so I found some scissors and when I was cutting it Phil told me they were fighting about if they should buy a KitchenAid or a Sunbeam mixer. I guess Steph bought the KitchenAid and Phil wanted the Sunbeam and when they got home Phil kept nagging her with his DJ voice until Steph finally came at him with the mixer. Anyway I cut Phils hair off and I was kinda shocked that he kept it mostly short after that and I guess I was kinda

proud too cause it was a pretty big change for Phil. But

the weird part about it all was Steph had short hair

before the fight but after Phil cut his hair off she grew

her hair long. I mean I dont know why thats weird or what

it really means but I remember thinking it was weird at

the time. Rosie said Chinese people have a name for that

kinda thing and its something about balance and harmony

but I never really saw nothing about balance and harmony

with Phil and Steph. I mean their marriage was pretty

much the opposite of balance and harmony and the truth

is they were probably better off apart and by that I

guess I mean divorced but I dont think Phil ever saw it

that way. Like I said after Steph left Phil didnt like to

be alone so he came to the house real regular. So I guess

thats why I wasnt surprised to find him kneeling in the

rose bushes the way he always was when I pulled up to the

house that morning after the Kings Head Hotel. I mean

Phil had his own house and his own yard and even his own

rose bushes but he mostly did nothing with them and the

truth was it looked real bad over there after Steph left

cause Phil spent all his time at my house with my yard

and my rose bushes. Anyway like I said he was there

kneeling in the rose bushes with a bloody thumb or something and he was curious about where I was last night so I said I was out with friends. Benny your fuckin friends dont stay out all night they work all night he said. Not last night I said. Last night we were at Orions Belt My Ass. I guess I should say Im not a good liar and I guess Phil knew there was probably something more to the story but he never said nothing else about it and that surprised me mostly. How about some hoops in the park today? said Phil and he snipped off a brown stem with thorns that looked like snake fangs or something and now his thumb was even more bloody than before. I dont think so I said. I guess he was a little shocked cause the truth was I wasnt real good at saying no to Phil neither but I dont know maybe the night with Rosie changed something in me. I mean I usually wanted to please Phil mostly but this morning seemed kinda different but I didnt really know why. What the fuck Benny said Phil. You roll in after a night out without me and now you dont wanna play hoops? I guess I grinned the way I kinda do when Im feeling nervous like the way I remember Ray grinned when the drug dog had its nose poked in the crotch of his cutoffs. Sorry I said but I got to see Ray today. Ray? said

Phil. Youre ditching me for Ray? Hes my brother I said

and I have to admit I felt a little weird saying it. Hes

your stepbrother said Phil. And you two are about as much

alike as a squirrel and a grenade. I wasnt sure exactly

what a squirrel and a grenade had to do with anything

but I figured Phil was trying to say Ray and me were

nothing alike and that was pretty much true. But even

when I was young I wanted to call Ray my brother. I mean I

always felt weird calling him my stepbrother cause

either youre someones brother or youre not so stepbrother

never seemed right to me. Ray treated me like a brother

mostly and by that I mean he beat me up lots and wrecked

my stuff but I guess he mostly stopped wrecking my stuff

after the American Flyer. He said model trains were gay

and only gays played with model trains and he stepped on

the locomotive and it exploded under his foot like it was

a land mine or something. I collected lots of beer bottles

and pop cans to get that locomotive so I was real mad at

Ray but when I went at him he pushed me down real easy

cause I was small for my age mostly and I didnt really

know how to fight at all. I told mom and she put out her

cigarette in a full ashtray and she cried and ran her

hand over my cheek and said with a real trembley voice Oh

Benny life is like that sweetie like that was supposed to make me feel better or something. I told Jack too but he already took a couple of his pills and it was like he was just looking right through me at the TV with x-ray eyes or something. I mean he lifted his leg and farted real loud but he always did that when commercials were on anyway so I didnt really count it as talking to him or nothing like that. When I told Truck the next day he went kinda crazy like it was his American Flyer locomotive or something and I mean he went crazy crazy like insane crazy. He got a Louisville Slugger from behind the seat of the Chevy and I followed him to my house real nervous all the way cause I didnt want him to smash in Rays head like he said he was gonna. I guess Ray saw him coming cause the front door was locked when we got there and Truck started hitting the door with the bat and I could see the dents he was making and thinking how mad Jack was gonna be about it and then Ray came to the window and did one of his ass-pancakes and I guess that was pretty much the wrong thing to do cause Truck swung at the window and broke a hole in it. It looked kinda like the hole in the ice where Elizabeth Kerns fell through and died the winter before but that hole melted in spring and the hole in our window stayed there covered with a piece of cardboard box for a couple of years after that. Anyway Truck ran away when he saw the hole he made in the window and I guess he knew there would be trouble when his dad found out and there was. I mean Trucks dad couldnt pay for the window so him and Jack mostly just yelled about it for a while then they went and got drunk at the Thirsty Bear Saloon cause Jack could steal draught beer there pretty easy while mom was working her shift. Truck got a few more broke ribs from his dad that night and I felt bad about it but I was glad he didnt smash in Rays head anyway. Like I said either youre a brother or you arent and I guess I decided that day that Ray was my brother no matter what. Anyway I left Phil in the flowerbed and walked to the curb to my two-tone Bel Air that I always parked on the street even though theres a paved driveway in front of the house. Phil parked his El Camino SS in the driveway mostly when he came by but I never parked in the driveway after Sam died. I dont know why for sure. I guess it didnt seem right somehow. Anyway the Bel Air was a classic but Phil said it was junk. Shit on wheels he said. Its only a classic when its fixed up Phil said. Just cause somethings old dont make it a classic Benny. But I thought Phil was wrong about that cause it was a classic even if the fender

wells were dented and the rusty front bumper hung

crooked. I liked the bumper cause it was kinda like a

crooked smile or smirk or something. So I drove the Bel

Air to Stop n Shop and I bought some double A batteries

for the radio I gave Ray last Christmas and a box of

Marlboro filters and a couple packs of menthol on the

side. Before I went in to the visiting room I took out two

packs of filters from the Marlboro box and put in the

menthols just like Ray said I should cause Ray liked

menthols but he said if the other inmates found them they

would beat him senseless or worse for smoking them fag-

boy cigarettes. When me and Tom Barron were still friends

before the whole Gus the dog thing happened he told me

that his uncle in England called cigarettes fags. I guess

thats why I kinda laughed when Ray said the thing about

smoking fag-boy cigarettes cause if Ray was in England

he would be saying cigarette-boy cigarettes and I guess

that wouldnt make sense mostly. Anyway Ray didnt think

it was funny so I never said nothing about fag-boy

cigarettes again. I gave him the box of cigarettes and the

batteries and he said thanks and I thought he pretty

much meant it. How are mom and dad? he said and I said I

didnt know the same as I always said. Ray knew I never went to see them mostly but he asked me anyway every time I came cause I guess it was his way of making conversation or maybe he really did wonder cause they sure never came to see him. Ray never left home like me and he lived there with mom and Jack until he was arrested. The truth is back then I went home some days when Jack was at the factory and used his tools to tune up the West Coast Vending van and it was one of them times that Ray was arrested. I was in the garage changing the oil filter and pretty soon the place was full of police and dogs and a big guy dragged Ray out of the house and put handcuffs on him and thats when the dog put his nose in Rays crotch. The other dogs were going crazy too barking and spinning around in circles so the big guy got a ladder and pulled down all Rays blocks of pot from the crawl space and I remember Ray said it was all mine but the police already knew it was his so he started to sob some and when they took him away he cried mostly and I felt kinda bad. Anyway that was the first time Ray got sent away to jail. The second was pretty much a year after he got out from the first time not long after mine and Sams wedding. Ray shook out a cigarette and lit it and said Ill be out in a couple of

months long as I dont kill no one in here. He laughed and
I laughed cause we both knew that if anyone in here was
gonna get killed it was Ray and not nobody else. He made a
funny kinda face and pulled a book out of his pants from
under his rear and I could see that it was a Bible so I
asked him why he kept a Bible in the rear end of his pants.
Well I aint reading it I tell you that he said. But I do
intend to start. So whats it for then I said. Protection he
said. I used to use it at night to cover the old bunghole
you know to keep the bum bandits away but now I just keep
it there all the time. When you hit the homestretch some
hillbilly is always looking to ream you on your way out.
Thats the way it is in the pokey little brother said Ray
and I guess I was surprised to hear him call me that cause
he never said that before. And I guess that made me think
that maybe we were grownups now and things were gonna be
different between me and Ray. Anyway I guess its fair to
say when I left the county lockup I felt pretty good about
me and Ray as brothers and I even thought maybe we could
spend more time together when he got out. It was kinda a
shocker to me too but thats what I was thinking when I
stepped into the gas and drove off in the Bel Air.

June 1

Ray, born Raymond Reed Kaczka to Jack Butler Kaczka and Rita Pakulski, was Benny's stepbrother. He wasn't hard to find. Ended up back in the state penitentiary for possession of marijuana with the intent to distribute. Habitual pusherman. Apparently, his bout with being a born-again Christian didn't stick. Seems he had a falling out with the good Reverend Grainger after the whole traveling revival thing imploded. Ray wasn't quoting scripture or using a Bible to protect his "bunghole"anymore. He agreed to see me for a carton of Camels, with two packs of menthols tucked inside, and some batteries for his transistor radio.

Interview Transcript: Raymond Kaczka

Me: So, I have to ask, how did you end up back in the state penitentiary?

RK: Bad luck, mostly, I suppose.

Me: Can you elaborate on that a bit more?

RK: Elaborate? Yeah sure. After I quit the reverend's revival show, I moved back to Dundee and got a job at Sonics working the drive-through window for minimum wage. Did you know that minimum wage is peanuts? Not really peanuts, but you know what I mean. It's a joke! I didn't know that, it being my first job and all. But it didn't take me long to figure out that I could make a lot more money, and I mean a lot more, if I was selling a little weed on the side. At first I just slipped a doob here and a spliff there into the food bag. Then after awhile I started making weed shakes. You know chocolate-ganja, vanilla-grass, strawberry-bud. Then I got this great idea. See, since it was coming up on Saint Paddy's day, I decided to make a mint-herb shake for the occasion. And let me tell you, it was a hit. There was a line-up all the way down Main Street for my mint-herb shake. Unfortunately, and here's where the bad luck comes in, I sold one to an undercover cop, an Irish cop, no less. Anyway, they found him dead in his car outside a 7-11 store a couple hours later. The car was full of chips bags, and Twinkies wrappers and pop bottles. I guess the cop got the munchies real bad, and he choked on a Dorito cheese chip. It didn't take the boys in blue long to track me down at Sonic. They tried to pin a murder rap on me but my lawyer got me off because like he said, I couldn't be responsible for the death of a man in an eating binge, even if I may have inadvertently caused the eating binge. So I pled guilty to a reduced charge: possession with the intent to distribute.

Me: Wow, that's quite the story. So you'll be here for another nineteen months, is that correct?

RK: And counting.

Me: How would you describe your relationship with Benny when you were growing up as stepbrothers under the same roof?

RK: How would I describe it? I dunno. It was normal, I guess. I mean we fought same as other brothers but overall, I'd say we got along pretty good.

Me: In his book, Benny recalls a few episodes in which you were quite cruel to him. For example, he wrote that you destroyed his American Flyer model train locomotive. Does that ring any bells?

RK: The model train… yeah, I remember that. But I never destroyed it on purpose. It was an accident. I'd been huffing paint and I was out of it at the time. I stepped on it by accident. But ol' Benny thought I did it on purpose and he starts going ape-shit. Next thing I know that nut-job Truck is bashing our door with a baseball bat, threatening to kill me and stuff like that.

Me: How was Benny's relationship with your father?

RK: My father? You ever met my old man?

Me: Actually, yes, I have. I've already interviewed him.

RK: Well if you met him, then you already know how his relationship with Benny went. In a word, not good.

Me: That's actually two words.

RK: Okay then. Here's one word: shitty. Same as my relationship with him. Same as everyone's. He never cared about no one but himself. Ever.

Me: So I guess it's safe to say that he doesn't visit you in here?

RK: Even if he wasn't retarded crazy or whatever the hell he is, he wouldn't come in here. From what I hear, he gets lost on his way to the shitter in his room.

Me: I'd like you to tell me about Benny's relationship with his mother.

[Before Ray can answer, a prison guard sticks his head in the door and says that visiting time is over.]

RK: Thanks for these. [getting to his feet, motioning toward the carton of cigarettes]

Me: I'll be back next week, if you don't mind.

RK: Suit yourself. Just don't forget my smokes.

The Thing that Happened At Work with Rudy

I drove to Tower Plaza and sat in the control room like I always do but things seemed kinda different and by that I guess I mean the gray screen I sat in front of didnt look so gray today. I remember I felt pretty much the same as I did when I first found Sam in the Motel 6 parking lot sitting beside the coke machine in her not sexy underwear. Maybe I looked different too cause Rudy stuck his head in the door and looked at me and I guess I smiled cause he came in and sat down. His eyes were big and black and they were glossy mostly like the way hard boiled eggs look right when you peel them so I could tell that he was sniffing floor wax again like he always did. The one time I went to Rudys apartment I saw cleaning stuff from work everywhere but the place wasnt real clean so I knew he wasnt using it for cleaning and it wasnt hard to figure out what he was doing with it. A few weeks before that I saw Rudy put some drops of toilet cleaner into a particle mask and he wore it around for a whole shift but when I asked him about it he just kinda grinned like he does and said it was his special blend. I got some coffee and sat down at the TV monitor and Rudy was just staring at me so

I asked him if he wanted some coffee and he said no. What do you want then? I asked. Nothing said Rudy unless you wanna come clean about what happened last night. I said nothing happened last night. I said I got in a cab and went home and watched Cheers and Barney Miller reruns and I went to bed like the way I always do. You got that look in your eye said Rudy. What look I said. The I got poon look he said. I dont know that look I said. Its the one sitting like a big fat hen on your face right now he said. Its like one of them smiles that twitches up and down cause you wanna smile but you know you shouldnt smile. I dont know what you mean I said. I mean you got poon on a spoon but you dont want no one to know about it cause you think you might jinx the whole works said Rudy. Poon on a spoon? I said. You know he said stuffing the sock hole. Wearing the fur hat. I got to go do my rounds now Rudy I said. Youll tell me some time he said but I ignored him and took my coffee and went to check the fire exits and they were locked just like they always were. Whenever I checked the fire exits I always thought about Truck and how after he got kicked out of school he got me to leave the fire exit of the school open so he could sneak in and steal stuff from the gym closet. At first I didnt know

what he did with that stuff and I felt bad mostly but I
guess by then I was kinda scared of Truck after what he
did to our house with his Louisville Slugger. I mean this
wasnt like spraying old Gusses coal hole blue. Like I
said me and Truck never did nothing terrible bad but I
guess you could say things were kinda getting that way
some. Anyway I found out later he was selling the stuff
cause he bought me a new American Flyer locomotive and
he got himself some brass knuckles too and he said he was
gonna knock his dads brains out real soon. I guess I knew
Truck was kidding mostly and he didnt kill his dad like
he said he was gonna but he beat him up real good and put
him in the hospital before he left town and never came
back. I guess that was just a few years before I left too
but I never broke no ones jaw before I left.

June 6

Looked for Truck's father to try and get him on record but couldn't locate him. No one around town wanted to talk about him, either. Was about to abandon the search when I found a local, Dundee pharmacist, Hal Fleischman. H.F. said he knew Truck's father–Theodore Sloane. People called him "Teddy." H.F. confirmed Benny's story about Sloane's wife leaving him, and living in the old Chevy truck for a summer. According to H.F., everyone in town knew Sloane's wife was having an affair except Sloane. When she left for Seattle to live with some pie-in-the-sky entrepreneur who planned to open a chain of coffee stores "named after some football player," no one was surprised except Sloane. Sloane took it badly.

B.'s story about Truck breaking his father's jaw before leaving town was basically true, too. If you throw in a few ribs, an arm and a cheek too. Fleischman knew this because he filled Sloane's prescriptions for codeine for months after that. When I asked what happened to Teddy Sloane after his son Truck left, the good pharmacist informed me that Sloane lived on the streets behind a dumpster out back of the Thirsty Bear Saloon for about a year. It was then that Sloane started making found art. Asked what sort of found art and H.F. curled his lips into a painful grimace. "Characters from the Andy Griffith show," he said, "made from beer cans and cigarette butts." According to H.F, the likeness was quite remarkable, but the characters were engaged in "all sorts of deviant acts… sexual acts." Teddy Sloane sold them on the streets for a quarter a pop. Until some vacationing New York City gallery curator, who'd decided roughing it on the West Coast was a good way to get in touch with his inner mountain-man self, bought one. A week later, Sloane was flying to New York first class for a big gallery opening. A gala event in the art world. "Haven't seen or heard of him since," said Fleischman.

I wanted to steer the conversation toward B., so I asked Fleischman if he knew Benny Salmon. He said, "Everyone knows everyone around here… it's just a matter of how well." Turned out Fleischman didn't know B. well. All he knew was B. was "the slow kid who painted the behind of Mrs. Crumley's dog, Gus." One thing that I'd heard over and over about Benny was he was slow–"retarded" was the word that most people used. Although I wasn't convinced that

B. did actually have some learning disability (I'd met him, after all), asked Fleischman if he knew what had happened to B. to make him slow. "No accidents that I know of," said H.F. "And Bea didn't start in with the bottle until after Marty left, so I suppose it was just a fluke–an act of God, I guess you could say." Nothing to add to that. Of course.

Thought I'd ask about Truck. "Do you know what happened to Truck?" I said. Fleischman gave me a look. It said, "You know I know what happened to him." But H.F. indulged me with an answer anyway. He told me everyone around Dundee knew "that juvenile delinquent would turn pro one day." You mean a criminal, I said to him, poised like a question to get him to continue. "Yeah, a criminal in jail." I mentioned that Benny had written a book. And that the book covers B.'s final encounter with Truck. H.F. said he read about it the papers. Everyone had. And Truck "got exactly what he deserved."

My shift was slow like most nights until I was watching the monitor and I saw Rudy lying face down in a hallway on the 16th floor. Rudy blacked out and stopped breathing a couple of times before so I wasnt real surprised but I was still kinda nervous. I mean I didnt want Rudy dying on my shift even though nobody liked him mostly but me and I only liked him sometimes cause I guess he was the only one in Tower Plaza that never talked to me like I was a moron or something. So far I brought him back with some mouth-to-mouth but I have to say I wasnt real happy about having to do that cause I got kinda light-headed just sniffing Rudys breath and he usually messed himself when he blacked out liked that. I knew how to do mouth-to-mouth cause the boss at West Coast Vending made us take a class about first aid after one of the other drivers died sitting in his van at a red light. His name was Gordo and he was eating peanuts from a cup in a cup holder and I guess some coins and stuff got into them and he choked on a dime. Traffic went around him for better than an hour before a police car finally pulled up behind the van and found out why it was just sitting there. I mean I didnt know how us knowing first aid coulda helped Gordo but our boss said we needed to be more fuckin responsible for each other and he signed us all up for the class and docked our wages the next six months to pay for it. Anyway I found Rudy and it was pretty much like I thought cause he wasnt breathing but his heart was kinda beating and he smelled real bad cause he messed in his pants just like I said he mostly did. I gave him mouth-to-mouth for a while but nothing happened and I thought his heart stopped too so I beat on his chest and got it going again but his breathing wasnt good so I thought I better call 9-1-1. I mean I knew Rudy would be mad about it mostly cause there would be lots of questions but I thought it was better than him dying right there in the hallway so I put him in the recovery position and put a blanket over him and waited for the ambulance. The emergency guys came and took Rudy away and said I probably saved his life when I gave him mouth-to-mouth and I felt real happy and kinda proud and I wanted to phone my old boss and West Coast Vending and thank him for making me take that class but I didnt. When I got home the next morning Phil was still there in the flowerbed and I thought maybe he slept there in the rose bushes. I was real tired and not in a real good mood mostly cause the thing with Rudy took a long time and

there was some extra paperwork and I never got over to
Orions Belt My Ass like I wanted to see if Rosie was there
again. I mean I couldnt stop thinking about her and the
night me and her had together and I wondered if she maybe
felt there was something special between us and not the
kinda special that you see on Hallmark cards or nothing
like that but the real kinda special. I mean I knew she must
see lots of different men but she said I was very special and
she really seemed to like suckling my man-boobs. Tonight
was my night off so I decided to go to Orions Belt My Ass
later and see if she was there but first I had to get some
sleep. I guess Phil wanted to talk cause he left the
flowerbed and followed me inside and asked if I wanted to
go to Big Boys for breakfast but I said no Im kinda tired
and I told him about the thing with Rudy. Fuckin waste of
space said Phil. Next time you should just leave him
there to die. I laughed like Phil was joking but I guess
he probably wasnt and then I said I had to get some sleep.
Oh said Phil kinda hurt some and he left and I think I was
asleep before his El Camino squealed out of the driveway.

June 15

Tried to contact Phil again. This time not at the station–followed him home. Thought I'd knock on his door. (Strangely, no rose bushes in front of his house.) His cherished El Camino (cherry red, no less) sat in the driveway. Noticed someone had keyed the passenger side door. A deep rage-filled gouge, at least a foot long. Guess you can only call someone a "douchebag" on air so many times before he retaliates.

Phil finally came to the door after the third knock (only because he'd never seen me before so didn't know who I was). Said he didn't want any "Goddamn pamphlets about Jehovah, His sheep, and whatever the hell it is he does with them." Said I wasn't one of them. "Then who are you?" So I told him. Half expected him to throttle me right there on his front steps, but he didn't. Instead, he looked nonplussed. Tranquilized. Like he'd been into the valium jar and it just then kicked in.

Asked him if we could talk for a minute. Said I understood that he and B. had a falling out, just wanted to know what it was all about. "What it was all about?" The look that suddenly commandeered P.'s nonplussed face was like he'd right then plopped down into a steaming hot tub right onto a sizeable prickly pear. In a flurry of incoherence, he said something about a black junkie whore and B. being her suckling sow. Stood and waited for the storm to pass. Then asked if he wanted to tell his side of the story. P. seemed to consider this. Hummed and hawed. Finally, he asked if I had a card. I didn't. But I jotted down my number at the Pinewood Lodge on a scrap of paper. He said he'd call me in a couple of days then closed the door.

What Happened When I Met Rosie Again

Mr. Fairfux says Im wandering some and not staying with the story mostly so I guess I should write about what happened when I saw Rosie again. I went to Orions Belt My Ass that night and Rosie was there but she wasnt there alone like last time. By that I mean she was with a man that looked like he was probably a fireman or a policeman or maybe a soldier or something cause he was real big and muscley like the way Im not. I sat at the bar where the farting Santa Clause was before but it wasnt there no more and the Christmas lights were gone too. The place was dark again like it usually was so I guess Rosie didnt see me sitting there like I was a storm cloud rolling in or something. I ordered a beer and I guess I was watching her real close and the truth was I was hurt some and jealous mostly even though I knew what she did to make money and I knew I shouldnt feel nothing like the way I was feeling. I guess right then I felt like the way I did when I was seven and sitting in the Thirsty Bear Saloon and eating a plate of French fries and gravy for dinner and watching mom serve boilermakers to loggers and fishermen and factory workers that bought her shots of tequila and squeezed her bottom. I knew she let them cause she needed a boyfriend real bad after dad pretty much up and left the month before. That was the first time I ever saw Jack cause mom called me over to the table and told me to say hello and I did and Jack told me to get him an ashtray and when I came back he butted his cigarette and took the ashtray and set it in front of him and he didnt say a word or even look at me like that ashtray just got up and walked there by itself or something. I remember missing dad real bad and missing that he used to take me to the garage on main street and let me hand him tools to fix cars with. He was tall and had shiny black hair and he tied his coveralls at his waist and crawled under cars in his white undershirt that never seemed to get dirty even though he had black smears of grease everywhere else. Then hed go to the till and take out five dollars and tell me to go get myself some ice cream and him some cigarettes from Wongs confectionary down the street. I didnt know the garage wasnt really his like he always said it was and the money in the till wasnt his neither and I guess that was why dad had to leave mostly. The real owner found out he was taking money from the till and I guess it was more than just money for ice cream and cigarettes

so he told me he had to leave but he would come back and

find me when he could but he never did. He said he was

gonna go to Canada to live like a big black bear in the

Rockies and no one would find him unless he wanted them

to. He said black bears always lived alone and he hugged

me real hard and went out the door of our house and I

followed him crying for a while until he finally told me

to get back home cause my mom needed me and he was right

about that cause I guess thats when mom started to drink

lots like the way I always remember she did. She cried and

drank and smoked at the kitchen table and let cigarettes

burn black scars into the table and then she went to work

at the Thirsty Bear and cried and served drinks and drank

and smoked and let cigarettes burn black scars into the

dirty red carpet. Anyway when the fireman or policeman

or maybe soldier reached over and gave Rosies bottom a

squeeze I started to feel kinda sick inside again and I

thought I might cry some like I did back at the Thirsty

Bear when no one was looking but I didnt. I drank my beer

and decided it was probably a bad idea coming to Orions

Belt My Ass tonight so I got up and walked out into the

street and I was coming up to my car when I heard someone

call my name. I turned around and she walked real slow
and her hips swung from side to side in a real short red
dress and shoes with heels that couldve nutted a Tsetse
fly like Phil always said. Where are you going lover? she
said. Home I said. You were gonna leave without even saying
hello? I said I guess I didnt see you but I knew she knew I
lied but she didnt say nothing about it. Well you see me now
dont you? Yes I said. Im looking for a date tonight she
said. What about the big muscley guy in there? I said cause
now I didnt care that she knew I was lying before. Donald?
Rosie laughed a little and her teeth looked real white
under the yellow street lamp. Hes just a friend. Ive been
waiting for you she said. Why? I said. Rosie came real close
and I could smell her skin and I could feel her breathing
on my neck. Cause youre special Benny. Remember? she said
and put a hand on one of my man-boobs. Oh I said like I
forgot or something but I really didnt. Lets go she said
and she got into the Bel Air.

I drove to the Kings Head and we got the same room as we
did before and it looked like no one cleaned it after last
time we were there. I guess it made Rosie kinda mad cause
she left the room and came back a few minutes later with

83

sheets and some folded gray towels. She gave me a towel
and told me to take a shower and she made the bed but
before I finished showering she came in too and washed
her woman parts and shaved her legs and armpits and I
have to say it felt kinda weird to me cause Sam sometimes
did that too. I guess I always thought showering was real
personal and no one else should see you washing your
parts or shaving or brushing your teeth or peeing like I
always did in the shower and like Sam always hated even
though I think she did it sometimes too. So like I said it
felt kinda weird but then Rosie washed my man parts and
it seemed okay and I guess I pretty much got excited right
away cause I started squirting man milk all over her and
all over the shower curtain. Rosie started to suck on my
man-boobs and I thought I might go crazy but not bad
crazy but good crazy. Real good crazy. The kind like when
youre just a little drunk and not lots drunk and
everything seems better than before. Thats the kinda
crazy I felt when Rosie did that thing with her tongue
and kinda chewed on my man-boobs with her teeth like she
was eating one of them tiny cobs of corn at the salad bar
or something. Rosie took me out to the bed and she laid me
down and sat on top of me and slipped me inside her and she

just sucked until my man-boobs felt numb mostly and I

finally shot. I guess I did better this time than last

time cause Rosie seemed real happy when we were done and

she just laid there beside me real comfortable and close

and licking her lips and not saying nothing. After a

while she got up and got a glass of water and took some

pills and said Im hungry Benny. Lets get breakfast.

June 16

Worked in the Lodge all day today. Transcribing interviews. Going over notes. Trying to get the arc of the storyline clearly in my head. And the angle. What was the angle? Not quite there yet. For someone in my line of work, it's a precarious place to be.

Thought I'd have a nip in my room before dining in the Pinewood Lodge Restaurant. The past four months I've eaten at every place in town. And surrounding towns. All basically the same. So why go anywhere when I can stay right here and eat a bloody elk steak under the watchful gaze of Bruce the Moose?

Couple of rusty nails later and I was ready to take on the world. Or at least the Pine Lodge Restaurant. The phone rang before I could get out the door. Don't know how, but I knew it was Gavin. Maybe because it was somehow dramatic. The timing. Me a little tipsy and just leaving the room for dinner alone. Gavin would've appreciated the theatrical value of that.

I answered. Heard the clear deep baritone voice that I'd always associated with strength. But it didn't sound strong this time. Gavin said Baby's Got Style had been canceled. Said he was thinking about leaving the city for a while. Going back to Missouri. He'd call me when he got there. I didn't know what to say. Didn't know how to stop him. Didn't know if I should try. All the crummy dialogue I've read and written over the years and I couldn't think of one lousy line to say. I knew then, at that moment, what I'd always suspected: eloquence is no stand-in for emotion, and wit is no match for honesty.

The line went dead before I could even say farewell. Before I could say anything. Somehow I felt like I'd missed it. The phone call. The show. Our relationship. Everything. Alone in outback Oregon, I poured myself another drink. Then another. Each one stiffer than the last.

What Happened When I Went to See Rudy and After That When Phil Decided I Needed a New Driveway

I dropped Rosie back in the city after me and her ate breakfast and I went to St. Michaels Hospital so I could see how Rudy was doing. For me it was a pretty big deal cause I never liked hospitals mostly and even when Sam worked for one I never went in past the cafeteria. Mr. Fairfux says its okay to write about when I was a kid and about stuff me and Truck did if it tells the reader something about who I am and why I act the way I do now so I guess here is one of them times. I never liked hospitals cause of what happened when I was ten or eleven. Me and Truck were stealing pickets from the neighbors fences so we could rebuild the deck of an old handcar we found down by the railway tracks. Truck said we should fix it up and get the hell out of town and it seemed like an okay idea to me back then even though I wasnt really thinking about getting the hell of town yet. So I took Jacks hammer and gooseneck from our garage and me and Truck pried loose a bunch of pickets and carried them down to the railway tracks. I guess we were fooling around and me and Truck stopped to pee in the bushes cause we drank a couple

bottles of Orange Crush each but then Truck tried to pee

on me and when I ran away I fell on one of the planks that

had a rusty nail sticking out of it. The truth is I sat on

it more than fell on it and I ran home crying all the way

and Truck called after me saying where the hell was I

going and calling me a baby. The nail hole in my rear end

got real red and the next day it started to hurt bad and I

guess I got a high fever pretty soon after that so I told

Ray about what happened and I showed him the hole and he

said I better get down to the hospital and get a tetanus

shot before lockjaw set in. I mean I didnt know what

lockjaw was but it sounded bad enough so I walked to the

hospital and waited till one of the nurses finally asked

me what was wrong and I told her the same thing I told Ray

but I was too shy to show her the nail hole so she took me

to a doctor and he looked and kinda clicked his tongue and

gave me a shot that hurt real bad. The nurse put me in a

bed and said she was gonna call my mom but I said my mom

wasnt home cause she was working at the Thirsty Bear

Saloon and she said shed call there instead. I dont know

if she really called mom but mom never came and I stayed

by myself in the hospital that night and I remember

being real lonely and scared and the next day I was
pretty much feeling better so I just left without saying
nothing to nobody. I got home and mom was sitting at the
kitchen table chain smoking and drinking coffee like the
way she did since dad left and she told me to hurry up
cause I was gonna miss school even though it was summer
vacation. I mean it wasnt hard to guess she didnt know
nothing about me being gone last night and so I never
said nothing about tetanus or the shot or the hospital
and I just went up to my room and slept and maybe cried
some too. Anyway when I walked into St. Michaels and got
on the elevator to the third floor I felt kinda lonely
like the way I did back then. It was one of them old
elevators and it kinda jerked lots and it didnt stop even
with the third floor so I tripped getting out. I looked
around for Rudys room and there were machines with red
and green lights all over the place beeping and flashing
so it looked like a real fancy garage or something. I
finally found Rudy in a room with three other guys that
looked about the same as him and he was watching one of
them daytime soap operas on the TV and he looked real
lonely sitting there by himself. I guess the real reason
I came to see Rudy was cause I knew nobody else would and

I didnt want Rudy to feel like I did when I was a kid in the hospital. I mean I knew Rudy lived alone and he didnt have any friends except for maybe me and I didnt think he had any family at least I never heard him talk about any. And I guess the truth was I couldnt really imagine what Rudys mom and dad were like cause it seemed to me like Rudy just kinda appeared here in this world full grown or something. Anyway I walked in and Rudy smiled real big like he was happy to see me and I saw that his front tooth was gone and there was just a big black hole there now. Benny my man my savior said Rudy and his breath kinda hissed in the hole and I felt embarrassed mostly but I smiled and said hey how are you feeling? He said the ambulance guys tell me you saved my life. No I dont think so I said. Well thanks anyway Benny he said. I guess I was kinda relieved to hear him say that. I thought youd be mad I said. Mad? he said. You might be in trouble at work I said. Naw Rudy said. No trouble. The new foremans a sniffer too. No worries. Oh I said like I didnt know that cause I pretty much didnt know the thing about his new foreman. You should quit sniffing I said. Yeah Benny I should he said. But Im not gonna sit here and lie to you cause youre like my only real friend Benny. Im not gonna

quit cause I really dont wanna you know? Its the only way
I can get through the day Benny. You know? he said. Yeah I
know I said and I guess I pretty much did. I asked him about
his tooth and he smiled again and said they dropped him
on the way in from the ambulance. Oh I said. Its cool he
said. All the codeine I want he said and he grinned and
pressed his tongue into the black space where his tooth
used to be. Oh I said. Anyway I better go. Rudy held out his
hand like he wanted to shake so I shook his hand even though
I didnt like the IV hose that was sticking out of it.
Thanks said Rudy. No problem I said.

I drove home and Phil was in the rose bushes again. I
thought it was kinda weird that he liked roses so much
cause he was supposed to be a real hard guy mostly that
didnt like nothing or no one. Mr. Fairfux says cynical is
the word Im looking for and I guess that sounds about
right. I mean Phil was hard on his radio show anyway.
Like I said I thought it was weird so I asked him about it
once and he said it wasnt the roses that he liked so much
but the whole growing thing like pruning and watering and
all that. He said he wished he knew about roses when Steph
was still around cause things mightve been different if

he did. The truth is I wasnt sure what he meant but I
guess he did so thats probably all that matters. I was
real near to being in the door cause I needed to sleep
before my night shift but Phil took my arm and pulled me
to the driveway and showed me some big cracks and one piece
of concrete that looked like it was sinking or something
and he said we have to fix the driveway. We have to tear
this son-of-a-bitch right up and pour a new one he said.
Okay I said but right now I have to get some sleep. Fuck
sleep said Phil. This is important. He went to the garage
and brought back the wheelbarrow and a sledgehammer
and a pinch bar and he said we better get started. So I
helped him break up concrete and carry it out behind the
back fence for a few hours. Phil talked lots and drank
beer lots and I mostly just helped but it felt good to do
something around the house even though I was real tired.
I was pretty much dead by the time I got to sleep and I
nodded off to the sound of Phil watching the Nature
channel downstairs. It sounded like a show about them
flowers that snap shut and eat everything.

June 23

I'm here with Rudolf "Rudy" De Sot at Portland Technical College, where he is studying forest management. His dorm room looks like that of any other freshman in college–desk, single bed, industrial carpet, beer and Bob Marley posters on the walls. But Rudy is not your typical freshman. For one thing, he's twenty-nine years old. I asked him about his circuitous route to college.

Interview Transcript: Rudy De Sot

Me: So how did you finally end up at college? The way Benny tells it, you were not long for this world, to put it bluntly.

RD: Well, yeah, he's so right about that. [pushes a low hanging dreadlock from his eyes]I was the huffmaster back then. [grins brownly, laughs hoarsely]

Me: And the poon-master, too, as I understand it.

RD: Yeah, man! [more hoarse laughter, then turning somewhat somber]That's actually not the total truth. My addiction counselor says I need to learn to be true to myself, and if I was being true to myself I wouldn't say that I was a poon-master. More like a poon-pretender.

Me: Well, we all tell ourselves little lies when it comes to poontang, don't we? I know I did–for twenty years. So don't beat yourself up too much about that. [uncomfortable pause] So what made you decide to seek help? Was it your last OD?

RD: Oh, no. I mean, Benny saved my life for sure, but I didn't quit after that. It was when I saw St. Francis. That's when everything turned around.

Me: You mean Saint Francis of Assisi? You saw a sculpture or a painting or something like that? Ribalta? Raibolini? Guercino?

RD: No man, I mean I saw him, spoke to him. Actually, listened to him. He did the talking.

Me: Oh, so you saw him in a dream?

RD: No. In the park. I saw him in the park.

Me: You saw Francis of Assisi in a park in Portland?

RD: Yeah, man, that's what I thought, too. I said to myself, right here in a park? But it was him.

Me: You do know that Saint Francis died in the thirteenth century, don't you?

RD: I know, I know. That's what made this so out there, you know. I mean Saint Francis [throws up his arms as if in praise] right there in the park. [pauses thoughtfully before continuing] Well, I mean it wasn't Saint Francis Saint Francis, you know? It was some kind of reincarnation of him.

Me: Okay. So how did you know that is was a reincarnation of Saint Francis?

RD: Well, he was dressed in some kind of plastic bag that looked like a robe or something, like the kind that Saint Francis wore, you know? And he was wearing a Snap On tools cap. That part didn't really make him look like Saint Francis but I remember thinking to myself that I hadn't seen one of those since I stopped visiting my uncle over in Canby. He ran an auto repair shop so he had one of those caps. I mean, Snap On doesn't just give those caps away to any slob on the street, you know?

Me: I didn't know that. So, he was wearing a robe or smock of some sort. What else? What made you think he was Saint Francis?

RD: Well, there were pigeons all over him and a couple of squirrels on the bench, too. And, I mean, he was talking to them, you know? And they were talking back.

Me: They squirrels were talking back?

RD: And the pigeons. [stops to reconsider] Well, not talk talk, but like talking some kind of animal language.

Me: And did he speak to you?

RD: Well, sort of yeah. I mean, he looked right at me and he kind of shuffled his feet and he started singing this song: "The forest is the place for me, the forest is the place for you . . ." And that's when it hit me.

Me: It hit you?

RD: Yeah, it hit me that I should protect the forests and that I should clean up my life and go to college. It was my calling from Saint Francis, you know?

Me: I have to ask, Rudy. Had you been huffing at the time?

RD: Yeah, sure, man. But that was my last time. I mean, I went to a rehab place and cleaned up and never did it again.

Me: Wow, that's a really terrific and somewhat inspiring story. Uh . . . but I'd like to know a little bit more about your relationship with Benny.

RD: Whoah! I mean, we were just friends, man. There was no relationship. [laughing nervously]

Me: Got it. But you went for beers together after work sometimes, correct?

RD: Yeah, but I mean that was all. We never went home together or nothing like that.

Me: Right, okay. Let's forget about the relationship part. Let's focus on Benny. Tell me about Benny.

RD: Benny? Benny was all right. Like I told you before–Benny saved my life.

Me: Was he like that? I mean, helping other people. Did he help other people?

RD: Yeah, I guess you could say that. I mean he wasn't giving people hundred dollar bills or anything like that. But he was always nice to people. He'd do stuff for them sometimes.

Me: Did you know his wife, Samantha?

RD: No, man. She was before my time.

Me: Did he ever talk about her at work?

RD: No, man. I mean, I never even knew he had a wife before until one of the other guys told me–told me she died, too.

Me: What about Norma–Rosie, I should say–you were there the night he first met Rosie, correct?

RD: Yeah, man. But I was pretty wiped. I don't remember much, except she was this nice black whore and Benny went home with her.

Me: Did you ever see her again after that?

RD: Well, yeah, I saw her with Benny a couple times at Orion's Belt, My Ass. And there was one time I saw her there alone, too. [pauses, smiles sheepishly] I guess I kind of hit on her. Because she's a whore and all, you know? But she shut me down fast and hard.

Me: Did you know that Benny experienced male galactorrhea? Male lactation?

RD: Male what?

Me: He began to lactate… secrete milk from his breasts… reportedly, after he met Rosie.

RD: Oh that. Yeah, I heard about that. Wow, that was crazy! I mean, he had a set on him, for sure, you know? Not double Ds or nothing like that, but his man-boobs were plenty big. Let's just say I caught myself staring at them a couple of times.

Me: Did he ever secrete milk at work–that you know of?

RD: No, man. I mean, I didn't even know that was happening till I read about it in the papers. The whole healing thing and what not. A real trip, that was.

Me: So, at the time, did you know that Benny was going on the road with the revival show?

RD: No, man. He just came into work one day and quit. He didn't say why–just said there was something that he had to do. I was cool with that, so I never asked him anything about it. I just figured he'd be back when he was finished doing whatever it was he had to do.

Me: How would you describe Benny to someone who'd never met him before?

RD: A good guy, nice guy. A real nice guy, I'd say.

What Happened When Me and Rosie Went to a Movie

When I was seven I had a purple banana-seat bike that dad
bought for me I guess with money he stole from the garage
I always thought was his. It had a real high sissy bar
and a fat racing tire on the back and I had a baseball
card of Carlton Fisk stuck in the front spokes cause dad
said he was a bum who couldnt hold a candle to Thurman
Munson. I didnt know but that sounded about right to me.
Anyway that summer I guess I was the most popular kid in
the neighborhood cause of my purple banana-seat bike until
Bobby Schwartz got a trampoline and then no one but Truck
wanted to ride my bike no more. And I guess Truck rode it more
than anyone else anyway and more than me too cause he just
came over and took it whenever he wanted and sometimes hed
keep it at the Chevy overnight like it was his or something.
Anyway for them three months of summer the other kids
really liked me. I mean I knew it was cause they wanted to
ride my purple banana-seat bike but I didnt care cause I
was mostly just happy they liked me even if it was just
for a while. And I guess I felt that way about lactating
and about Rosie too. She really took to the teat just like

the old saying says and I dont really know why for sure. I
guess maybe it was cause she did everything else before
like I mean all the different positions and all the weird
stuff but she was never with a lactater before. I mean Im
kinda guessing about that but Im pretty sure she never
was so I was just happy she liked me mostly even if it was
just for a while. And that was the real truth with lots of
mustard on it cause the boloney is sliced real thin as my
dad used to say. I guess what I mean is I was happy to be
with her and near someone. Three gray and silent years
was enough so I guess you could say I became a regular
customer of Rosies.

In the next couple of weeks me and Rosie met pretty much
every night and we always ended up back at the Kings
Head Inn. So I guess it would be fair to say we had lots of
sex. I mean good sex like good and normal kinda sex but it
always ended with Rosie suckling at my man-boobs and
staring up at me with big round eyes. I guess the truth
was they were kinda scary eyes in a way but not monster
scary but more like worried scary kinda looking like
they were looking for something but I didnt know what
exactly and even if I did know what they were looking for

I probably didnt have it anyway. After a while me and
Rosie pretty much stopped having sex and went straight
to the suckling part. I dont really know how to explain it
but the suckling part was better than the best sex we ever
had. I dont know I guess it was kinda churchy or something.
Like something coming from somewhere deep inside but from I
dont know where exactly. Mr. Fairfux says that rapturous
might describe the way I felt when me and Rosie were suckling
so I looked it up and thats pretty much it. Anyway the first
time it happened was maybe three weeks after the first
night at Orions Belt My Ass. Me and Rosie took a taxi to
the somewhere in the east end of the city instead of the
Kings Head Inn and Rosie took me up the rusty fire escape
of this four-story brick building. She never told me
where we were going but she said it was a surprise. I mean
it didnt really look like a hotel or nothing and I guess it
was some factory or something a long time ago. Anyway she
took me inside and I found out that it was her own place
where she lived so it was kinda a shocker. I mean not the
place itself cause the place was real normal and real
kinda womany I guess like I could tell a woman lived
there with fat candles and long mirrors and pictures in
frames and dishtowels folded in half and orange juice in

a pitcher and stuff like that. Anyway I guess I was so

shocked I didnt know what to do so I tried to put some

bills into Rosies hand cause the pay was always upfront

before but this time she told me to keep it. She said buy me

breakfast in the morning and she took off her jacket and

long black boots and sat down on the sofa and covered her

legs with a yellow and orange afghan. And I said okay and

I guess I was smiling real big cause I knew that maybe I

wasnt Rosies customer no more but I was something more

than that now. So me and Rosie stayed up until morning

talking mostly and she told me how she came to the city to

be an actress and she laughed kinda embarrassed like it

was an inside joke or something and it pretty much was an

inside joke cause I didnt get it. Rosie told me about her

family and they sounded real normal. I mean normaler

than my family cause her dad never left to live like a

black bear in the Rockies and her mom never married

someone like Jack and she never had a stepbrother like

Ray who smoked pot and did ass-pancakes and all the rest

of it. I guess I thought she was kinda like Sam and her

real normal family. But now I think about it Sam and

Rosie werent really the same cause Sam was a nurse and

Rosie was a prostitute and them are two pretty different

jobs. But they were both kinda real tender and they both took care of people I guess and they both seemed like they could break pretty easy. I guess the thing that I thought was really the same was they could break pretty easy. Mr. Fairfux says what Im trying to say is they were both vulnerable and I guess hes pretty much right again and I guess thats no surprise cause hes better at saying things than I am. I mean at first I thought Rosie was kinda hard like the way you think a prostitute is but now I think she wasnt so hard mostly but she just wanted to seem that way. Like the same way that Phil wants to be hard on the radio I guess. Anyway that night was when Rosie told me her name was Norma not Rosie. Rosie is just my work name she said. I have to say it was a bit of a shocker to find that out. A real shocker. I mean the part about her telling me her real name was a shocker but also her real name being Norma was a shocker too. I guess I wasnt surprised that Phil made a joke about it when I told him later. He said the only Normas he knew needed mustache wax and liposuction. It was kinda funny at the time and I guess he was kinda right cause Rosie didnt look like any Norma Id ever seen either except maybe Norma Jean like she was a kinda beautiful black Marilyn

Monroe or something. That would be about right I guess.
Anyway we were both real tired but we just couldnt seem
to stop talking like we had to say all these things
tonight cause after tonight we might not be able to or
something. Like this was some kinda special deal that
only lasted one night like the way midnight sales last
all night and people start lining up at sundown and when
the doors open they shop all night for stuff they dont
need just cause its cheap. Anyway the next morning I
bought her breakfast like she said and later when I was
ready to leave she stopped me and said there was
something more she wanted to do. So she took me to this
movie theater. I dont even know what the movie was just
some old war movie I guess. It was black and white and
scratchy and the sound was real bad. Anyway we found a
seat near the front and there were lots of people around
but we sat down in the middle of them anyway. The gray
pictures were flashing on the screen and pretty soon
Rosie started to suckle and by that I mean she pretty
much ripped my shirt open wide and my belly kinda pushed
up and was all swollen from the 18 wheeler omelet I had
for breakfast and she started pulling and sucking at my
man-boobs like the way she liked to do. I mean I could tell

people were looking at us and maybe watching us more
than the movie even. But Rosie didnt care and I guess I
didnt care cause my man-thing started pressing hard
against my fly and pretty soon my man-milk was running
down her chin and it looked real white in the dark kinda
shining there on Rosies dark skin. I just stared at her
and smiled mostly even though the people around us were
talking and whispering real low. And now I guess that
time in the theater kinda changed me I think and it
changed Rosie too cause we never had sex again. Like I
said after that we just suckled all the time. Anyway I
dont really know how it happened but I remember looking
down at Rosie suckling there and the sound of an old
airplane made the movie speakers buzz and some guy on the
screen was saying goodbye to his girl and she was crying
and I was thinking I loved Rosie or Norma. I mean that was
the real shocker. It was crazy but not crazy crazy like
Uncle Bo living alone in the woods crazy but good crazy
like yipping puppy crazy or something. Like I said I
wasnt really looking for nothing like that. But then
there it was the plain truth and the simple truth rolled
into one bigger plain and simple truth I guess. I loved
Rosie and that was pretty much that.

July 1

John F. called this morning. Said he's going to be "out of town" this weekend and wants an update on my progress. Out of town? In book-industry-lingo that translates to "spending the holiday week-end drunk in Florida." Told him things were moving along—although a bit slower than I'd hoped. Told him I'd originally planned to be back in NYC for the holiday. But I won't make it. Instead, I'll be watching fireworks from the relative yet lonely comfort of the Pine Lodge Veranda, sipping on drugstore champagne, and listening to celebratory gunfire off in the distance. (Didn't say this.) He thanked me for taking on this "special project." Yes, John F. thanked me! I thanked him back. Said B.'s was a fascinating story. He agreed. Said it was going to be a massive best seller. Said the first print run is 250K. At that point, my heart skipped a beat or two and my stomach sprung into my throat like that bell and hammer game at the carnival. 250K! Oh, the pressure! I'm sure I stammered before finally getting the words "Don't worry" out. Guess that's what he wanted to hear because that's the last he said about it.

Could tell he was about to hang up but decided to say one more thing. Said he was sorry to hear about Gavin's production going under. To say I was terribly surprised by this is a colossal under-statement. Had no idea John F. even knew Gavin existed, let alone knew about his play. "Oh" was all I could think to say. Asked if he'd seen the play. J.F. said "Of course, yes." He'd gone to see it on the recommendation of a friend. Said he'd even made it backstage and met Gavin there. Was all very confusing to me and I must've sounded very confused because J.F. took this opportunity to get off the line. Leaving me wondering if the world could really be that small.

July 2

Spent the day in my room making phone calls. Trying to track down Rosie. Her name is either Norma Fitzsimmons or Norma McCully. Not sure which one yet. Working on it.

What Happened When I Poured the Driveway with Phil
and Later When I Visited Ray

The cement truck came real early Saturday morning cause Phil knew the guy and he said hed stop by before his real work started on some apartment building in the city and give us some cement for free. I could tell Phil was real happy and I guess he liked the idea of some rich apartment owner in the city paying for my driveway. The fuckerll be none the wiser said Phil. Getting screwed by the little guy he said and smiled. We fixed the cement forms with stakes the Saturday before so the driveway just kinda sat there all week like four empty apple boxes but bigger. I mean it wasnt like the driveway meant anything mostly but I guess I felt like it kinda meant something cause it was like I was moving on or something and leaving Sam behind. I even thought maybe I was like one of them sicko serial killer guys who buries the body and pours a cement floor over it or something. Not really but I remember thinking about that and thinking that the body would always be stuck there and that was real creepy but I guess maybe that was the point. I mean it wasnt like I was burying Sam under the driveway or nothing like that but it felt like I was changing the place and maybe she wasnt as much a part of it cause of that. Like I said before I never parked in the driveway after Sam died and I guess it was cause it was too much like going home and I didnt wanna go home cause Sam wasnt there so I parked on the street like I was a guest or something. Anyway the cement truck came and Phil was wading around in the hip waders I used to use for fly fishing until I found out how hard it was and I was no good at it so I quit one day. Phil was shoveling cement into the corners like he really knew what he was doing and I guess he pretty much did cause after the truck left he got out a trowel and a straw broom and finished the job while I watched mostly. I thought the least I could do was buy him breakfast so we got in the Bel Air and drove to Big Boys. Me and Phil ordered the 18 wheeler omelet like we always did and thats when I told him about Rosie or Norma. I have to say I wasnt sure which name to use yet so I stuck with Rosie mostly cause using Norma seemed kinda weird to me and it felt kinda private or something too. Phil wasnt real surprised when I told him I was seeing someone but I guess he picked up on the name Rosie pretty much right away cause he looked up and

kinda scrunched up one eye like he was driving without
sunglasses or something and said Rosie? Shes either fat
or black or a whore he said. Or maybe a fat black whore.
Just a black whore I said. Shes not fat and her name is
really Norma I said. Thats when Phil said his thing
about liposuction and mustaches. Then he got this kinda
proud look on his face and he said thats right Benny!
Leave it to the professionals! Thats what I do he said. I
know I said. You do? he said. Yeah I said. How? he said. A
guy at work saw you in Koreatown I said. Anyway shes not
a professional when shes with me I said. Phil looked at me
with both eyes scrunched up this time like the way you do
when youre looking right at the sun or something. What
do you mean? he said. I mean me and Rosie are more than
that I said. More than what? he said. More than prostitute
and john I said. John? he said. What the fuck? Is this an
episode of Hill Street Blues? Who the fuck says john when
theyre not actually talking to someone named John? he
said. You know what I mean I said. She took me to her
apartment and I bought her breakfast the next morning.
So youre saying shes really your girlfriend he said.
Yeah I guess I said. Bullshit Benny he said. I know whores
and they dont have boyfriends he said. Thats why theyre

called whores he said. So then I told him how Rosie
thought I was special cause of my lactating. Bullshit
Benny he said. The only thing whores think is special is
money. Take my word for it he said.

I stopped and bought Ray batteries and his usual box of
cigarettes and I stuck two packs of menthols in it the way
he liked but today when he came out and sat down behind
the Plexiglas he said he didnt want them. I have to say it
was a real shocker cause Ray started smoking cigarettes
when he was twelve and before that he smoked twigs off
the ground. When Jack and Ray came to live with me and
mom Ray was smoking packs of cigarettes he stole from
Wongs Confectionary mostly but sometimes he would pick
up dry hickory sticks and smoke them too. He said he used
to do it all the time when he was a kid but now he was older
he liked cigarettes like an adult did. So I smoked a hickory
stick with Ray but then I threw up tuna sandwich on my
shoes and I never did it again. Anyway I asked Ray why he
quit smoking and he said he found the Lord and I have to
say that I was confused by this cause I didnt know what he
meant at all so I said what do you mean? I found the Lord
Jesus Christ he said and he sat real straight and proud

like the way you do when you just got a ringer in
horseshoes or something. You mean he was lost? I said
cause I thought it was kinda weird to say that he found
the Lord cause I didnt think the Lord was lost but I did
think he wasnt around too much these days. No Benny he
said. I was lost and the Lord found me. So the Lord found
you and not you found the Lord I said. Yes Benny thats
right he said. The Lord found me. Okay I said but I still
wasnt getting where the smoking part came into the picture.
And the Lord dont want you to smoke? I said. Thats right
Benny he said. The body is a temple and a temple cant be
smoky he said. I didnt know that I said. You being a simple
sort theres lots you dont know especially about the Lord
he said. Yeah I suppose I said and I knew he was right
about me being a simple sort cause everyone I ever knew
said that about me and I knew he was right about the Lord
cause mom pretty much never churched us when we were
kids or nothing like that. I guess the only thing I knew
about the Lord was what I learned from the Jehovah
Witnesss pamphlets they stuck in the door and I didnt
read them mostly but I sometimes looked at the pictures
and I thought Jesus looked real friendly and kinda
handsome too like maybe he could be starring in his own

movie or something and now Im older I guess I think he really is kinda starring in his own movie. Anyway Ray brought out his Bible like before but this time he didnt pull it out of the rear end of his pants. He looked at me real serious and said all the answers are in here. In the Good Book he said. But I thought the Good Book was only good for keeping the bum bandits in here away I said. Benny Benny he said like I said something real dumb even though it was something he said himself before. I have no fear of the bum bandits no more he said. The Lord is with me he said. Oh I said and I thought about the handsome Jesus on the pamphlet. So the bum bandits leave you alone now? I said. No he said. The bum bandits plug my bunghole every night he said. I have to say this was a real shocker. I mean Ray was pretty much always worried about being a fag or something even before he got sent up the river. Mr. Fairfux says the word Im looking for here is homophobic and some people dont like the word fag but Im just saying what Ray was always saying so I hope them people understand. Anyway like I said it was a real shocker so I said Dont you care about your bunghole being plugged no more? Ray told me about one night a few weeks back when the bum bandits came and he fought and fought but they got the Bible out of his pants and they plugged his bunghole again and again for pretty much the whole night. According to Ray the Bible fell open in front of him and while they were plugging his bunghole he kept reading one verse over and over. Genesis 44:13 said Ray. It was like a beam of light from on high just lit up that verse he said. It glowed he said. Ray leaned in close and whispered through the little holes in the Plexiglas. Then they rent their clothes, and laded every man his ass, and returned to the city he said. And every one of them convict bastards laded my ass that night just like the scripture says they did he said. Ray smiled but not like a real happy smile but like the kinda smile you get from your friends at work when the boss just fired you for something and you know you deserved it mostly. I have to say that pretty much none of it made sense to me like the bunghole plugging and the verse and all that but it seemed to make sense to Ray cause I never really saw him like that before. I mean I saw him kinda relaxed and calm before but that was only after spending an afternoon in the crawl space of the garage smoking pot and this was a different kinda calm and relaxed than that. I guess it was like Ray knew something for sure for the first time in his life and I guess that made me feel happy for him mostly and I thought about telling him about Rosie cause she made me feel happy too but I didnt. Thats good Ray I said. Not the bunghole plugging part I said but the other part. Praise the Lord. It sure is he said. I guess I kinda smiled cause Ray said thats what good Christians say you know. I didnt know that I said. And Im a good Christian now thanks to Reverend Grainger he said. Ray told me Reverend Grainger came to the prison every Sunday and had a meeting for the convicts so they could feel like they werent worthless and God loved them. That man of God changed my life Benny he said. Thats good Ray I said and he said no Benny youre not getting it. Im a changed person he said and I thought maybe he was cause he seemed real different to me. Reverend Grainger says God can change any man he said. And then Ray told me about Truck. I have to say it was real shocker to hear the name Truck cause after I left home I never actually heard anyone say his name again. I mean I thought about Truck sometimes and I wondered where he was and what he was doing but I never heard anyone talk about him. Even old Truck was changed by the reverend said Ray. Hes born again just like me he said. Truck is here? I said. Ray smiled big and

this time it wasnt the smile like when you just get fired
but the smile like when you know something that someone
else dont and it makes you feel all high and mighty or
something like the way the guy on Jeopardy smiles all
the time when someone gives a wrong answer cause hes got
the right answer on a card right there in front of him.
Yep hes in here said Ray. And he said to say hello to you.
Whats he in for? I said. Armed robbery he said. A
convenience store somewhere upstate. But now hes found
the Lord too said Ray. Praise the Lord. Yes praise the Lord
I said. How longs he got left? I said. Well thats the good
part of the story said Ray. You see Reverend Graingers got
some pull around here and hes getting me and Truck and
all the other convicts who found the Lord out on early
release. Im out in two months and Trucks out in about the
same said Ray. And he wants to see you when he on the other
side he said. That is good news I said and I guess it was
but I wasnt sure about seeing Truck again cause things
were lots different now than when were kids. And I have to
say the news about Truck finding the Lord or I guess the
Lord finding Truck was real crazy too and the hard to
believe kinda crazy cause I have to say I dont really
know if thats good crazy or bad crazy. I mean Truck never

cared for nothing mostly when he was a kid but churches were always something he pretty much hated so I guess it seemed kinda weird that now he was part of one. I remember how me and Truck broke into Holy Cross Church one night and Truck climbed up into the organ chamber and did a dump in one of the big pipes. It was pretty much the talk of the town for a while cause everyone was saying how the next Sunday the low G pipe shot out a stool that hit the ceiling and stuck there and the pipe never played right after that cause the low G always made a kinda fizzling sound and the whole church stunk real bad when the organist played Handels organ concerto in G minor and I guess that was his favorite so he liked to play it lots. Anyway I wasnt sure what to think about seeing Truck again or about the Lord finding Truck so I left the prison that day feeling weird mostly about the things Ray told me. But I guess the feeling didnt last too long cause I knew I was gonna see Rosie after work tonight so I stepped into the gas and watched a puff of blue smoke rise from back of the Bel Air and it made me feel better doing it mostly same as it always did.

July 4

Tried to call Gavin at his parent's home in MO. His mom said he was supposed to be there by the holiday weekend but he never showed. She assumed he'd stayed in NYC—said in such a way as to ask for my reassurance that he had indeed stayed in NYC. Said "Yes, I forgot. He made some last minute plans with friends. That's where he is." Felt bad for lying but worse for not knowing the truth.

Hung up and immediately tried Gavin's apartment. Got the answering machine. Said nothing after the beep. Nothing at all.

July 12

Called on the Wilkes at their home tonight. Felt I hadn't got the information I wanted from Sherman at the Righty Tighty. S. said they were eating dinner. Asked if I could wait inside. He said they'd just finished dinner and were doing dishes. Said I'd help. Said I just wanted to talk. Ellen looked concerned. Maybe even frightened. S. finally shrugged and pushed the door open. Followed them into the kitchen and slid onto a padded stool. Asked if we could talk about Sam. S. tossed a dishrag. Said as long as you work while you're talking.

Interview Transcript: Sherman and Ellen Wilkes

Me: In a word or two, how would you describe your daughter, Samantha?

SW: Kind and generous. [looking to Ellen, as if for answers] Intelligent . . . but also . . . complicated.

Me: Kind and generous I understand. What do you mean by complicated?

SW: Oh nothing, really. That was in her younger days. She got over it.

Me: It?

SW: Nothing. I don't want to talk about that.

EW: She used to . . . cut herself. [Ellen exhaled the words as if she'd been holding her breath for ten years] She was sixteen when I first noticed them. Tiny slices with a razor blade on her arms and legs, like she was counting the days or–

SW: [interrupting] But that all ended when she met Benny. She stopped when she met Benny.

Me: So you believe that Benny was good for Samantha?

SW: In some ways, yes, I guess you could say that. He made her happy. That much was true. [sneaking a glance at Ellen] But in other ways he wasn't so good for her.

Me: So you would say they had a good marriage?

SW: I guess that would be fair to say.

Me: I can't help but get the feeling you don't like Benny much? Was it because he was a security guard? Maybe you would've rather had a Doctor or an MBA for a son-in-law.

SW: [chortling through two cavernous nostrils] No, it was nothing like that. I would have taken care of them for the rest of their lives, so long as Benny made Sam happy. It didn't matter to me that he was a security guard.

Me: After the funeral, you didn't see Benny much. Is that correct?

SW: He came around with Philip a time or two. But not much, no.

Me: So you didn't try to remain in contact with your son-in-law after the death of your daughter. Perhaps it was too painful to see him. Would that be a fair assessment?

SW: [tipping his head down thoughtfully] Well, yes. It was painful. How could it not be? But there's more to it . . . more that you don't know about. Because it's doubtful that Benny could've told you even if he'd wanted to.

Me: Can you tell me, then?

SW: No . . . no, I don't think so.

EW: Sheldon . . . [placing a wet hand on his sleeve and leaving a hand print] maybe you should try. Just try.

SW: [breathing deeply, scratching his head] Well...it's like this... Sam had...woman problems...plumbing problems. We'd known about these problems since she was a teen–and maybe that's why the cutting started. It's hard to say for sure. Anyway, the doctor said she could never have a baby, so we'd done our best to prepare her for that. But after she married Benny, she wanted a baby.

EW: [growing agitated] I tried to talk sense to her, but she wouldn't listen.

SW: And when Sam got pregnant, we tried to talk to Benny. Explain to him how dangerous it was for Sam to go ahead with the pregnancy and have the baby. But he just couldn't understand…

EW: [squeezing a tear from her eye] He was too simple to understand. No common sense . . . [her voice trailing off like a final wisp of smoke into the night air]

SW: And Sam wouldn't listen to us. [picking up a plate and buffing it in an endless circle of futility] She went ahead, even though she knew the risks. I guess she thought it was worth it. But was it really worth it? Well, I think we all know the answer to that question now.

When I first arrived at the Wilkes' home, I had a lot of questions for them. But they'd vanished into some fog of irrelevance. No longer seemed important. And somehow I felt ashamed. Ashamed that I had come into their home and pried painful answers from them, like snagging them with a hook then yanking that hook out of their mouths. Just like a good researcher should. Got the full story. But now I wasn't quite sure what to do with it.

**What Happened with Me and Phil in Big Boys and me and
Rosie in the Coffee Shop and Later at the Police Station**

After the time at the movie theater me and Rosie started
to suckle outside mostly and by outside I mean in public
places. Like I said before we pretty much stopped having
sex but we were suckling all the time now and suckling
outside in public made it real exciting I guess. Mr.
Fairfux called it ex-something and said it meant people
liked doing things like that in public places but I have
to say that at first I wasnt real happy to suckle in public
but Rosie seemed to like it so I went along with it. But the
truth was Rosie more than liked it and I guess I was happy
to be with her and I woulda done pretty much anything she
asked me to if it made her happy cause like I said before I
fell in love with Rosie that morning at the movie theater
and I knew it for sure now. I tried to tell Rosie at the
theater but it didnt seem like the right time then and
there didnt seem to be a right time after that neither. So
I guess what Im saying is I didnt tell Rosie how I felt
ever. Even after everything that happened with Ray and
Truck and Reverend Grainger she never knew how I felt

about her and how she made me feel and now I guess maybe

shell never know. But Mr. Fairfux says I shouldnt talk

about that yet cause that comes near the end of the story

so I guess thats all Ill say about it for now. Anyway me

and Rosie started suckling outside in a bunch of public

places. When I told Phil about it he said What do you mean

outside? Like outside the bedroom? Like outside in the

kitchen? That kinda outside? We were at **Big Boys** like we

pretty much always were and Phil was poking the pointy

end of his toast into a yolk that kinda rippled mostly

but didnt break. No I said. Like outside the house in

public. Phil did that thing with his Adams apple again

and I thought he was gonna spray coffee all over the

booth. So breast feeding youre whore girlfriend isnt

enough now you gotta breast feed her in public? he said. I

knew it wasnt a real question but I nodded anyway. So where

in public? he asked. I told him pretty much everywhere.

Phil kinda frowned. So wheres everywhere? **Be specific** he

said. He finally punched a hole in the yolk and was

soaking it up with his toast. So I told him about the

theater and about how we had suckled on the front row

when an old black and white movie was playing on screen.

Okay. Weird but not super weird he said. Where else? In

the park I said. Which park? he said. Livingston I said.
Kinda busy he said. And I said Yeah it was. Where else? he
said. In the public library I said. Ive seen worse there he
said. One time I swear I saw a guy going down on the Easter
bunny in the public library. I heard Phil tell that story
before but I didnt say nothing. So where else? he said. In
the St. Catherines I said. Wait! The cathedral? No! Thats
just wrong Benny. So wrong! he said. I know it I said.
Youre gonna go hell he said. I probably am yeah I said.
Then Phil got all serious like I never see Phil get. You
gotta stop Benny. You know I love you like a brother and
Im glad to see youre moving on but Im telling you as a
brother and a friend you gotta stop. He picked some egg
from his mostly blond goatee. I asked him why. Why? Are
you fuckin kidding? Where do think this is gonna end? he
asked. I said I didnt know. He said I better think about it.
He said I better find myself a real relationship. Then
something came over me and I dont know what but maybe I
just wanted to say it out loud to someone even if that
someone wasnt Rosie so I said I love her Phil. I guess this
time there was pretty much no stopping it cause Phil
sprayed coffee all over the booth like he was the broken
handle of a two-bit carwash or something.

Me and Rosie drove into the city and found one of them five-dollar-coffee coffee shops to suckle in. It had lots of windows and wood counters and floors and there was no vinyl and carpet like **Big Boys** and no waitresses walking up and down the aisles with pots of thick black coffee that looks like the kinda sludge that leaks from your oil pan. The place was full and loud but still seemed quiet mostly and I dont know how that was but maybe it was cause some of the people there were reading books or writing in their laptops computers. I mean I only ever saw a laptop up close once and I pretty much never saw anyone read a book except for in school a time or two and so I have to say that it seemed kinda weird to me that people were reading on their own in the coffee shop. Anyway me and Rosie bought fancy coffee with stiff foam and brown cinnamon and found a place by one of the tinted windows and some song was playing in the speakers. Someone to watch over me it said slow and breathy and it made me feel more tired than I already was. Rosie took off her big round sunglasses and set them on the table and she sipped her coffee real slow. I guess I was staring at her cause she said Benny are you flirting with me? and I didnt know what to say so I just sat there all red and smiling like the way you look when your favorite aunt catches you peeking up her dress or something. Then Rosie slid over close to me and the next thing I knew she was running a hand inside my jacket and squeezing my man-boobs. She didnt have to rip my shirt open no more to suckle cause she already cut holes around the nipples of my suckling shirts and now my nipples looked like two pink antennas or something sticking out when she opened my jacket. Pretty soon Rosie was suckling and I guess she was moaning kinda loud cause some people closed their books and laptops and took their five-dollar coffees and got up and moved. But some stayed and watched cause I guess they never saw nothing like that in a fancy coffee shop or maybe any coffee shop before. The music was slow and smoky even though there was no smoking allowed and the woman was singing theres somebody Im longing to see I hope he turns out to be someone to watch over me and at the same time I was touching Rosies hair real soft and she was suckling at my man-boobs and I was thinking that maybe it was me that was the somebody that was supposed to be watching over her. Anyway pretty soon the manager came over and he was a young guy with real short hair and real big ears and I thought maybe he

should be out delivering papers instead of managing a
fancy coffee shop. He asked us to leave but I have to say
that he wasnt really asking so much as telling and he
said he was gonna call the cops if we didnt get out of
there. That just made Rosie mad mostly and she wiped her
mouth and said we werent doing anything wrong. Nothing
against the law anyway she said. I wasnt real sure if
what we were doing was against the law or wasnt against
the law so I decided it was best if I didnt say nothing at
all. Anyway Rosie just started suckling again and the
manager watched for a minute before he walked away real
mad and his brown pants made a kinda swooshing sound
like the kinda sound you hear when someone is sawing wood
in the backyard or something. Anyway I watched him
behind the counter and he opened his cell phone and he
was talking to someone and looking real mad like the way
Mrs. Szazadni used to look in sixth grade when Truck
crawled out the window of the classroom in the middle of
English class and the rest of the kids just pointed and
laughed lots. That kinda mad. So pretty soon a policeman came
and Rosie groaned when she saw him and she straightened up
and wiped her mouth and I closed my jacket so my nipples
werent showing no more. Rosie said the policeman. I

should have known he said. Officer Dalton said Rosie kinda formal but not real friendly. What brings you here? said Rosie. We got a call said Officer Dalton. Something about some sex act in a public place he said. That public place being here he said. No sex act here said Rosie. No sex act at all she said. Whos the john he said and I thought of Phil and what he said about Hill Street Blues. Hes not a john said Rosie. Then what is he said Officer Dalton. Hes my man said Rosie and that made me feel real happy inside. Your man? said Officer Dalton. You mean your dealer or your pimp? he said. He doesnt look like a dealer or a pimp. Hes no dealer and hes no pimp said Rosie. Hes my man. My boyfriend. Officer Dalton laughed some like the way Phil laughed when I told him Rosie was my girlfriend. Whatever you say Rosie. Look he said. The manager here is complaining. Now I dont know what you were doing but it was causing trouble said Officer Dalton. So if you wanna go downtown you just keep on doing whatever it is you were doing. Otherwise you better vacate the premises he said. Am I making myself clear?

Me and Rosie drove out of the city back to her place in the

Bel Air. I had one hand on the wheel and one hand on

Rosies thigh and I guess I was driving kinda slow cause

people kept passing and honking real angry like but I

didnt care cause Rosie was there beside me and I was her

man. Her boyfriend. I have to say I was still feeling real

happy about what Rosie said to Officer Dalton about me

and I guess that pretty much put me in a talking mood. So

whats it like? I asked. Whats what like? said Rosie. You

know I said. What you do. Rosie turned and looked at me and

the sun was just setting and the light seemed kinda lazy

just bouncing off her bare shoulders. You mean turning

tricks? she said and I thought Phil might say something

about Hill Street Blues again if he heard Rosie say that.

I nodded and Rosie pulled her knees up to her chest and sighed

real loud like she was getting ready to say something big and

I have to say this hit me hard and pretty much knocked the

wind out of me cause I remembered it was the same way Sam

sat in the Bel Air and sometimes sighed too. I guess I

looked confused some or real sad or something cause Rosie

said You okay Benny and I said Yeah Im okay. Then Rosie

sighed again and told me about how she started turning

tricks when she came to the city. Like I said before the

dancing thing didnt work out for her and she needed

money real bad. I dont wanna lie to you Benny she said. I

did lots of bad things in those early years she said. Like

bad bad or crazy bad bad? I said and she laughed and said

like bad bad I guess. I stuck needles in my arms Benny she

said. I was a junkie. An addict she said. But I quit all

that and Ive been clean for over two years. I have to say

that this was a real shocker. I mean I knew there were

people who did drugs and stuff like Rudy did and I guess

like Ray did too but I didnt think too much about that

cause I thought everyone can do what they have to do mostly

to get through the day. I guess I just didnt see how someone

could stick needles in their own arms especially cause I

still remembered how much the tetanus shot in my rear

end hurt like crazy when I was a kid like crazy bad bad.

The truth was I didnt like to do nothing like that at all

and sometimes I came real close to throwing up when I just

cut my fingernails. Mr. Fairfux says that makes me

squeamish and I guess hes right about that too. Anyway I

thought about what Officer Dalton said about Rosies

pimp so I asked her about it. Theres no more pimp said

Rosie. Im what youd call a free agent now she said. But

there was a pimp once? I said. Yeah there was said Rosie.

He wasnt really that bad as far as pimps go. Not like the

kinda guys you see on TV with fur coats and platform

shoes she said and I have to say that I was pretty much

thinking of that guy exactly before she said that. So he

never hurt you? I said and Rosie kinda curled tighter

like she was cold all of a sudden or something. Sometimes

she said. But not as bad as some of the others she said. It

made me feel sad mostly and maybe angry some too when she

said that. Sad like the way I felt the first morning after

dad left to live like a black bear in the Rockies. I guess

its the same kinda sad I felt when Sam and Becky died too.

Its the kinda sad that can never be fixed cause you cant

go back and change it at all. I mean I wanted to change it

and the truth was I tried for a long time to believe I

could change it but then I finally gave up and I guess

that was probably the saddest day of my life. Sadder than

the thing that made me sad in the first place. You know

what I mean. Anyway I guess Mr. Fairfux would say Im

talking myself in circles so Ill just keep moving on with

my story. Me and Rosie went back to her place and I made

her my chili con carne waffles like the way I made them

for Sam with onions and peppers from our garden except

Rosie didnt have a garden so we stopped and bought onions

and peppers from Super Saver Groceries instead. Rosie watched me in the kitchen like she thought I was crazy but good crazy not bad crazy cause she never heard of chili con carne waffles before and I said that was cause I invented it myself. I dont think dishes are really invented she said. Not like the light bulb or the computer she said. Yeah I guess not I said and she said but the idea was definitely yours. Ive never heard of anyone making chili con carne waffles before. So I put two waffles on a plate and scooped chili con carne onto them and poured real sweet maple syrup over the whole thing and told Rosie how I first came up with the idea. Jack and Ray pretty much moved into the house a month or so after dad left. I was still missing him real bad and I guess Mom was too cause she was drinking lots more than usual down at the Thirsty Bear Saloon where she worked. Most nights there was nothing fixed for dinner and that wasnt real unusual cause the truth was Mom wasnt much of a cook and she worked most nights so most of her time in the kitchen was spent smoking and making coffee and maybe burning a grilled cheese sandwich or something every so often. Anyway one night after Jack and Ray moved in and Mom was at the Thirsty Bear like usual and

Jack was sitting real dull in his green chair in front of the TV with his opened pill bottles beside him and he told Ray to tell me to make him something to eat. I have to say that I was used to making my own dinner so I guess I didnt think much of it when Ray came into my room and told me Jack wanted something to eat. Ray was eleven then and just about three years older than me so he was lots bigger than me and his voice was kinda squeaky but still rough maybe from all the twigs he smoked. So I went down to the kitchen and looked around to see what was there but it was like I already knew there was nothing. The fridge was empty except for some bottles of beer and a small bottle of Louisiana hot sauce and half a bottle of Aunt Jemimas syrup and in the back was something black that used to be an apple or onion or something round. I took out the hot sauce and the syrup then I looked in the freezer and found two frozen waffles. I guess I could have just made waffles for Jack but I decided to take a look in the pantry just in case and there was nothing but an old tin can with no label and a bottle of pickled beets. I took a chance and opened the can and it was chili con carne that looked okay so I put it on top of the waffles and gave it to Jack. Like always Jack never said nothing and he never really looked at the chili con carne waffles cause he ate them while he was watching MASH. I decided they must have been okay cause Jack ate them all and never said nothing bad about them not even to Ray. Anyway that was how it started. I made them again and Jack ate them again and every other time after that too. By the time I met Sam I guess I was getting pretty good at making my chili con carne waffles cause after she tried them she wanted me to make them every Sunday night. So I did. Rosie came up behind me and rested her chin on my shoulder. Thats the first time youve ever talked about your wife she said. I know it I said. Im glad you told me a little about her she said and I knew when she said it that Sam would like Rosie if she were still here. I dont know how I knew it but I did and that made me feel not so sad when I thought about Sam being big and pregnant with Becky and sitting at the table Sunday night eating my chili con carne waffles. I set two plates piled real high on the table and said come and get it. And she sat down and ate all my waffles till the plate was clean just like the way Sam did.

July 23

Took a trip to the Seattle West precinct to talk to Officer Dalton. Fortunately, he was working behind a desk and was amenable to an interview. Officer Dalton was not big and broad with a buzz cut like the kind of cops you see on TV. If it weren't for the uniform I wouldn't have thought him to be a cop at all. Maybe a bank teller or a shoe salesman. He got us two Styrofoam cups of coffee and set them on the desk. Then he leaned back and waited.

Interview Transcript: Officer Jerry Dalton

Me: Thank you for agreeing to speak with me. As I mentioned on the phone, I'm researching for a book and your name comes up in it.

JD: Well, that makes me wonder what kind of book it is! [his snigger is a slightly too-high titter, just on the verge of full-fledged laughter]

Me: You may remember one of the main characters, a working girl named Rosie.

JD: Yeah, sure, I remember Rosie. Haven't seen her in a while. Maybe she finally cleaned up and went home. Or didn't clean up and went to Hollywood. She talked about Hollywood a lot.

Me: It sounds like you were quite familiar with Rosie.

JD: What can I say? I work vice. Comes with the territory. I know all the working girls.

Me: Did you pick Rosie up often . . . for soliciting, I mean?

JD: In the beginning, yeah. Back then she was mixed up with a pimp named Hector. A real bad seed. Used to rough her up a lot. I remember picking her up one time, and I mean really picking her up . . . off the street. She had two black eyes and a broken cheekbone. I really thought she'd pack it in and go home after that. But by then, she was already hooked on the junk.

Me: You said in the beginning. How was that different than later?

JD: She eventually got away from Hector and became a renegade.

Me: A renegade?

JD: An independent . . . a girl without a pimp. I guess she worked up the exit fee and got herself free of Hector.

Me: So you didn't see Rosie much after that?

JD: Oh, I saw her enough. I just didn't bother picking her up. She wasn't what we call "toxic." She wasn't out there poisoning the streets. As a renegade, she spent most of her time working the bars.

Me: Like Orion's Belt, My Ass?

JD: Yeah, that was one her regular haunts.

Me: In the book I'm working on, there's a scene in a coffee shop, when Rosie introduces you to her boyfriend. Do you remember that occasion.

JD: Occasion? Ha! Yeah, I remember. How could I forget. Her and the guy were doing some kinky stuff and cleared out the coffee shop. I mean, I've seen just about everything imaginable when it comes to sex with strangers, but that one was a new one for me.

Me: But he wasn't a stranger. He was her boyfriend.

JD: So she said.

Me: You didn't believe her.

JD: Look, these girls have more boyfriends than I've got pimples on my ass, excuse my French. Maybe he was, maybe he wasn't. But I guarantee you one thing . . . he wasn't her only boyfriend.

Me: You mentioned earlier that Rosie had dreams of going to Hollywood. Can you tell me more about that.

JD: What's to tell. They all had a dream of being somewhere other than here–most of them dream of Hollywood. Nothing more to tell than that.

Me: So you know where her hometown was?

JD: Yeah, Coeur d'Alene.

Me: Idaho?

JD: That's the one.

Me: And how did she end up in Seattle?

JD: The way I understand it, she moved to Seattle to live with her Aunt. Her mother and father put her on that bus then they joined some death cult in Montreal.

Me: A death cult?

JD: That's what I heard. I don't know anything more than that.

Me: And did you know her real name was Norma?

JD: Norma McCully, yes.

Me: And you don't know anything about her whereabouts or her condition now?

JD: No. Why would I?

Me: You haven't heard what's happened to her?

JD: No. Should I?

The Thing I Found Out When I Went Home the Next Day
and the Funeral After That

I got home and Phil was waiting on the steps with a beer
and bloody fingers from being in the rose bushes again.
He told me Ray called from jail and that was real shocker
cause Ray never called from jail before. When he wasnt in
jail he sometimes called and just burped or farted real loud
into the phone or something without saying a word but I
always knew it was him cause I could hear him giggling his
stoned kinda giggle. Ray says you better call him as soon
as you get in said Phil. I guess I knew it was something
bad cause like I said Ray never called me before so I went
inside and called him. Rays voice was low and kinda shaky
and he told me that mom died last night. What do you mean?
I said. I mean she died Benny he said. Shes dead. Was she
hit by a car? I said. No Benny she wasnt hit by a car he
said. What do you think Benny? She drank herself to
death. She died sitting at the kitchen table smoking a
cigarette he said. Oh I said. Where was Jack? Ray sighed
real slow like I said something I shouldnt have and said.
He was watching TV in the next room but the police say he

never heard a thing. Oh I said. Dont worry Benny said Ray. Shes gone to a better place. Shes with the Lord now he said. I guess so I said cause I didnt know what else to say. And Benny? he said. Yeah I said. Can you pick me up tomorrow? Reverend Grainger is getting me out a couple weeks early on account of this family tragedy said Ray. What time? I said.

I drove to Rosies that night and she knew something was wrong as soon as she saw me. I guess I was crying or looked like I should be crying or something. Oh Benny she said and she took me in her arms and pulled me inside her apartment. What is it? she said. My mom I said. She died. Oh Benny she said. Im so sorry. Rosie led me to the sofa and sat me down then she hooked her legs over mine like she always did and covered us both with the afghan. Were you close to her? she said. No I said. I havent seen her really since I left home. A couple of times maybe I said but pretty much just on special holidays kinda thing. But that dont mean you didnt love her said Rosie. No I guess not I said. Tell me about her she said. So I told Rosie about mom and some real old memories from when I was a little boy. I told her how mom and dad met when mom was riding across the country on a crazy bus with lots of crazy hippies and by crazy I dont mean crazy crazy I mean drug crazy. I guess the bus broke down cause the clutch burned out and when the hippies took it into town it was dad who fixed it up. He was under the bus dropping the tranny so he could unbolt the clutch housing and I guess the hippies were sitting around on the grass outside the garage smoking marijuana cigarettes and singing their hippie songs about peace and love and such and thats when he heard the pure and simple voice of my mom singing something about flowers and going to San Francisco. He rolled the creeper from under the bus and stood staring at her in his coveralls tied at the waist and his clean white undershirt with his black hair combed back. Dad said it was like his life was pretty much a dirty old pair of boots or something and mom right then kicked the mud off them. They got drunk and stoned together and slept under the stars that night and the next morning the bus left without mom and I guess it was something that she never let dad forget cause she always talked about missing the bus and blamed him for it. But I dont think dad was bothered by it mostly cause he said she missed that bus on purpose and shed do it all again given the

chance just to be with him. Rosie liked my story about mom
and dad and she said it was real romantic and I guess it
kinda was in a way. I felt better just talking about mom
and I guess that was what Rosie was hoping all along.
Them were the happy times I said. Before dad left. I think
mom was real happy then I said. Rosie ran her finger over
my chin and stopped it right there in the small cleft
that Ray always said made me look like an ass-face and
said then just think about them. The happy times she said.
I thought I might kiss her just then but Rosie reached
behind the couch and got a bag and she said she bought
something special she said. She took a blue checkered
long-sleeved shirt from out of the bag and held it up
against my chest. Perfect fit she said. I noticed that the
nipples were already cut out of the shirt and the holes
were stitched real nice with red thread so I guessed that
this was a shirt we would wear to go out suckling on the
town. Do you feel like getting out of here said Rosie. Yeah
I said. Then put this on she said and I did.

I got to the state penitentiary and Ray was waiting outside
the front gate. I have to say that he looked like a changed
man mostly standing there with a paper bag of his

belongings in one hand and his Bible in the other. This

was not the Ray I knew and grew up with that was for sure.

Ray got in the Bel Air and threw the bag in the back and

set the Bible there between us like it was something that

we were needing to have a talk about sooner or later and I

guess the truth was that suited me fine cause I thought

if the Good Book could do that for Ray maybe it could do

something for me too. It wasnt that I felt I needed changing

exactly but just that maybe I was needing something more

churchy in my life. Mr. Fairfux says that at the heart of

the story lies my quest for trans-something to a more

spiritual plane and I guess maybe hes right about that

but I have to say that when me and Rosie suckled I got a

real spiritual kinda feeling and Mr Fairfux says

precisely yes although Im not sure why or what he means

by that. Anyway I asked Ray where he was headed and he

said he didnt know. I thought maybe he misunderstood me

and he thought I was asking him about his big plans in

this lifetime so I asked again in a different way this

time. Where do I drop you off? I asked. Drop me off he said

although it sounded more like a question than something

he said. Why Benny I was thinking I would stay with you

for a while he said. I have to say that this was a real

shocker cause I never thought Ray would wanna stay with

me. I guess I thought hed stay with one of his pot-

smoking friends from jail or something. Oh I said. Okay.

The truth was I didnt mind Ray staying at the house

mostly especially now that he was a changed man but I

guess I was worried some about how Phil might see that

since he pretty much stays at the house too. But still I

couldnt say no to Ray cause he was my brother after all

even if Phil said he wasnt really my brother except in

name and I guess that was pretty much the same way as me

and Phil are still brother-in-laws too. I decided to see

how Ray felt about it so I asked. Ray I said. Do you think

of me and you as brothers? He got this funny look on his

face like the way you look when you have to put wet

undershorts back on after youre already dry. Of course I

do said Ray. Who could be more brothers than we are? I

half smiled and said yeah youre right but I guess deep

down I still wasnt really so sure.

Me and Ray drove the Bel Air the two hundred or so miles

back to our hometown the next day. I guess Phil didnt

wanna ride with Ray so he said hed see us at the church

and he took the El Camino and drove there by himself. Me

and Ray went down main street past the garage where dad
used to work and past Wongs confectionary. Farther down
was one of Sherms hardware stores and the Thirsty Bear
Saloon. It was kinda a shocker cause it looked the same as
always except a little older. I guess it was just repainted
so it looked more shiny than normal in the noon day sun
but there was still the blacked out windows and the big
thirsty bear out front with a half pitcher of beer in one
paw and a full mug in the other. Me and Ray got to Holy
Cross Church and I have to say that it was a real shocker
again cause Father Owens was still there. I guess I never
thought about it before but he pretty much came right
from the seminary to Holy Cross Church so I guess he was
still a young man mostly back then even though he seemed
real old to us. When he saw me and Ray he came forward and
a white hand poked from somewhere out of his black robe
and I took his hand and shook it. Im so sorry for your loss
boys he said and I thought maybe he shouldnt call us boys
no more cause we were men now but then I thought he was
probably just thinking we were still moms boys or
something. The truth was Father Owens tried real hard to
get me and Ray to come to Sunday Mass when we were boys
but it just never took with us although mom put on a

dress and went now and then when she wasnt too hung over and she was feeling trodden down by life I guess. This way boys he said and he led us to a room where a big black coffin was open. Why dont you take a moment to say your goodbyes he said and then he walked away with real soft steps and I wondered if it was his funeral walk or if he always walked real soft like that. Ray went right up to the coffin like there was nothing to it but I wasnt so sure I was ready to see the dead body of my mom. I mean I never saw a dead body before cause the only other funeral I ever went to was Sam and Beckys and they were both cremated although I did see a dead horse in the middle of Flanagans field once. It was Truck that took me to see it. He picked up a stick and moved the tail so I could see the big hole where the horses rear end used to be. It was real big and bloody and Truck told me aliens landed right there in Flanagans field last night. They fucked this poor horse to death said Truck. But I knew the horse was a gelding and I said so. Thats right said Truck. Them stupid aliens didnt know no better so they fucked him anyway and thats sure as shit what killed him he said. Look what they did to his poor arse said Truck. He clucked his tongue real loud like it was a real shame. I followed him around to the horses head and there were ants going

in and out of its nostrils and flies buzzed around its

shiny black eyes some. Look at that said Truck. Look how

his eyes are open wide like hes real surprised he said.

Them aliens mustve snuck up behind him and fucked him

before he knew what was happening. Truck jabbed his stick

into the horses eye but it bounced back mostly so he did it

again and this time it broke and a bunch of water and

blood leaked out. I guess I didnt believe Trucks story

cause I asked Ray about it when I got home and he said

Truck was an idiot. Some fox ate the ass out it said Ray.

Thats all. Aint no goddamn aliens Benny he said. Aliens

or not that dead horse stayed with me over the years and

its something I remember real well still. Anyway I

decided to take a look at mom so I took a few steps forward

and I peeked into the coffin and saw her skin was white

and powdery and her hair was brown mostly with a bit of

gray and real thin too. I have to say she didnt look

peaceful to me like the way they always say dead people

look in their coffins. I was waiting for Ray to say

something about something about it like Jesus she could

have used a wig or Christ almighty she looks like a

hagridden whore or Goddamn they shouldve buried her

with the bottle but he never said nothing like that and I guess that goes to show how prison and the Good Book changed Ray. It was about this time that Father Owens came into the room and he turned around like he lost something on the way and a minute later Jack came walking in real slow like if he walked slow enough he could miss the whole thing and go back to his recliner in front of the TV or something. He looked up and saw me and Ray and he walked to mom and put a hand on hers and he stood there for a while. Me and Ray sat down and waited and I guess it hit me that maybe Jack loved mom in his way and that he was gonna miss her. After five minutes of just standing there Jack backed away from the coffin and sat down beside Ray. Pretty soon Phil came in and a few others that I remembered from the Thirsty Bear Saloon and the funeral started and was pretty much over before I really knew it. Father Owens was going on about mom being in a better place and Ray kept saying Amen out loud and holding up his Bible and Father Owens didnt seem to like it mostly but Ray kept doing it anyway. When it was over Phil gave me a kinda half hug and even shook Rays hand and I guess it was then that Didier the cook from the Thirsty Bear Saloon came over. His beard was combed and real long like

I never remembered seeing it before cause he always had
it tied tight in a knot under his chin when he was working
in the kitchen so he wouldnt dip it in the deep fryer or
singe it on the grill. I mean back when I was a boy it was
real black and kinda frizzy but now it was pretty much
smooth and white like ribbons or something. Real sorry
about your mom said Didier. She was one of a kind he said
and then he put something in my hand and when I opened it
I saw it was moms Hawaii bracelet. I guess it kinda struck
me that Didier was right about her being one of a kind. I
mean when I was a boy I knew mom wasnt like other moms
cause she didnt cook and iron clothes and clean the house
and she left the bathroom door open when she peed and
sometimes she put sour milk in her coffee even though she
knew it was sour. But she was different in other ways too
like the way she wore that Hawaii bracelet. I mean mom
never went to Hawaiithats for sure. She bought the
bracelet at a garage sale and she wore it pretty much
every day for a year when I was in grade one. I remember
cause Julia Grisak asked me about it one day in class and
I told her mom came from Hawaii and my grandpa and
grandma moved here to the mainland when she was a little
girl and my mom wore that bracelet the whole time after

that cause she didnt wanna ever forget where she was from so she never took it off. I guess what made it worse was mom didnt wear any other jewelry like rings or earrings or necklaces. The truth is I think getting dressed in the morning was hard enough for mom without being bothered with other things like jewelry and such but then one day the bracelet just disappeared from her wrist and I dont know why but I thought she just lost it or something. I never guessed there was more to it than that like maybe she wore it cause she wanted to go there someday but one day she realized she was never gonna go there so she just took it off. Didier smiled and his brown teeth glowed some like dingy gold or something. She gave it to me some years back he said. Lots of year back, actually. She said it wasnt doing her no good so I might as well have it said Didier. I thanked Didier and I put the bracelet in my pocket and thats when Ray came over and gave me a piece of paper folded in two. Whats this? I asked. Its a will said Ray. Whose will? I asked. Moms will said Ray. Mom had a will? I asked. Seems so said Ray. Whered you get it? I asked. Dad said Ray. Jack had moms will? I asked. Seems so said Ray. Are you gonna read it or not? asked Ray. So I opened it and

read. It said when I die have fun. Go out and get drunk. Go
bowling. Remember me. Love Mom.

Country Lanes Bowling was busy like it always was on
Saturdays and there wasnt an open lane nowhere in the place.
I guess Father Owens had some pull with Wes Standish cause
he got the owner to clear out some leaguers for us on account
of moms last request I guess you could call it. We rented
shoes and Jack went to his locker and took out his own
shoes and ball. I guess bowling was something Jack took
up after I left cause I never knew him to do nothing
besides watch TV. Me and Phil carried bottles of beer back
to the table and Father Owen sat at the scoring desk
scribbling down names. I have to say that it wasnt fun
like the way mom probably wanted it to be cause I guess no
one really wanted to be there mostly but we bowled anyway
cause we thought we should. Didier downed two bottles
before he got up and threw a strike and Jack came next
with a spare that took some skill to pull down and then
Ray threw one in the gutter and said something about no
bowling alleys in the pokey but no one laughed so he threw
another one and clipped the seven and then everyone laughed
real loud. Phil laughed loudest but then he got up and

threw a four-eight combination so he didnt do much

better than Ray. I took a long drink from my bottle and

got up and threw a strike without any trouble at all and

that was something cause the truth is I was never much of

a bowler. I guess I tried too hard like I could get the

pins down just by thinking about it or something. I know

enough about bowling to know that good bowlers pretty

much just let it happen and I remember thats what dad

told me once too. He sat me down with a Mountain Dew and he

bowled a game by himself while I watched. Let it happen

Ben he said. The pins wanna fall. They just need you to let

them he said. Then he got up and took two steps to the line

and released the ball and let all ten of them pins fall

with a loud crack. I mean he looked like a ballet dancer or

something and I dont mean in the gay kinda way like Ray

would say with the tights and all that. Dont ever try too

hard Ben said dad when he walked back and sat down. Thats

what most people do. They just try too damn hard. So like I

said I guess that was me. I tried too hard and so I never

liked bowling much but today things seemed different

than before and I just let the pins fall like the way dad

said to. I mean I think even Jack was impressed with my

game although he never said so. When the game was done we

left Father Owens lying on the bench snoring real loud
cause he drank a couple too many beers for a man of the
cloth I guess.

Me and Phil decided to stop and see Sherm and Ellen cause
I never saw them after the funeral at all and Phil didnt
see them much more than that neither. So I told Ray to
take the Bel Air home and I rode with Phil to the big house
with the Cadillac still parked in the driveway and the
two tall weeping willows on both sides of the front lawn
that always made me sad but I dont know why. I have to say
that I was real nervous about going cause I guess I never
felt Sherm and Ellen liked me mostly when Sam was alive
so it seemed plain enough to me they wouldnt like me at
all when she wasnt alive. I mean I know they didnt blame
me for what happened to Sam and Becky but I guess they
maybe thought if Sam had a different life and maybe
married a different man and had a different Becky then
she would be in a different place and time and that maybe
the story would end different too. And the truth was I
thought it sometimes too. Im not a real deep thinking man
at all but it just seems these things pop into your head
when youre sitting there wondering what happened and

where everything went wrong. Sherm and Ellen seemed

happy enough to see us and Sherm said Hey boys real loud

like he always did and Ellen hugged us both and she

looked like maybe she was gonna cry some. Me and Phil

followed them into the living room and I saw the two urns

on the mantle of the fireplace and I knew right away they

were the ashes of Sam and Becky. I guess they never asked

me if I wanted the ashes and I never asked if I could have

them so there they were looking kinda lonely and sad and

I guess right then I knew why the weeping willows out

front always made me feel sad. There were lots of pictures

of Sam in the room but only one of me and Sam together

from our wedding. I mean it wasnt something that I thought

should bother me and it didnt mostly except I guess I started

missing Sam again when I saw all them pictures and pretty

soon it felt like there was no air left in the room or something

cause I couldnt breathe right. It was like the way you feel

when youre a kid at the swimming hole and youre holding your

breath underwater for a long time and you finally burst out

of the water and you cant seem to get air into your lungs fast

enough. Me and Phil stayed for some coffee and cookies but we

said we couldnt stay for dinner and pretty soon we were

leaving. I mean I thought it was weird that we never said

nothing about Sam or Becky the whole time we were there. I
guess Moms funeral put me in the mood to talk about them
and how they disappeared from my life but every time I
was about to say something I saw something like dread in
Ellens eyes and I knew she knew I was about to say something
and she didnt want me to so I didnt. I just sat there and
listened to Phil talk about his job and lie about how he
and Steph were getting back together soon and this seemed
to make Sherm and Ellen happy mostly. So we said goodbye
and Sherm and Ellen made me promise to come by again soon
but I guess they didnt mean it cause I knew they felt
awkward some the same as me and I decided it was better
for us to keep our thoughts and memories about Sam and
Becky separate from each others. Bye boys said Sherm real
loud and me and Phil waved from the open windows of the
El Camino and pretty soon they disappeared behind us and
all I could see was the two weeping willows getting
smaller in the distance.

August 1

Took a trip down to the Thirsty Bear Saloon today. Pretty much the way B. describes it: dark, gloomy, void of all hope or any sense of optimism. Where men and women come to confirm their deeply held convictions that life stinks. Just another tavern. Surprisingly, Didier is a bit of a bright light in this alcohol-induced limbo. A beacon, of sorts. When I first met him I immediately sensed he wasn't one to wallow, to worry, to wish for more or better. Talking to him, it was clear he lived in the here and now, a space as cluttered or as clear as we want to make it.

Interview Transcript: Didier Serges

Me: Thank you for taking a few minutes out of your busy day to speak with me.

DS: [says nothing but smile pleasantly and nods]

Me: Benny Salmon has written a book, a memoir of sorts, detailing the past few years of his life. I've been assigned to help him write that book, so I'm trying to find out as much as I can about the things he talks about in his manuscript. Have you heard anything about his book?

DS: Not about the book . . . but I read about him in the Times. Like everybody else around here.

Me: Benny mentions you when he talks about the funeral of his mother, Beatrice. Did you know her well?

DS: Bea? Yes, I knew her well. We worked together for a lot of years. You can't help but get to know somebody well when you spend that much time together. [laughing]

Me: [laughing] And yet many a husband and wife manage to. [more laughter] The details Benny gives about his mother in the manuscript are rather sparse. Do you know much about her past?

DS: I know she was on a Greyhound from St. Louis bound for Seattle when the bus broke down and left her stranded here. She met Marty at the garage and never left. Never made it to Seattle.

Me: So she wasn't a Merry Prankster?

DS: [looking confused] A what?

Me: A hippie . . . on a cross-country road trip . . . on a psychedelic bus.

DS: She was no hippie. She was headed to Seattle to pick strawberries in June.

Me: Oh, well, it seems Benny didn't quite have his facts straight.

DS: That may've been what she told Ben, but that's not the way it really happened. She tried to protect Ben as best she could.

Me: What was it like working with Beatrice . . . uh . . . Bea?

DS: Well, there were good days and bad. I'm sure you know about her problems with the bottle. I'm not going to lie to you, some days it was hard to watch. Especially having dragged myself out of the same predicament.

Me: Oh, you're a reformed alcoholic?

DS: Seventeen years, four months, twenty-eight days sober. And counting. Quit the day I walked away from the merchant marines. Haven't looked back since, on either of them.

Me: Did you ever try to help Bea stop?

DS: You've never known an alcoholic, have you?

Me: I don't know, but I think I may be borderline myself.

DS: If you ever knew a real alcoholic, you'd know that nothing you can say will ever make them quit. And part of being an alcoholic is avoiding people who would want you to quit. Bea trusted me not to do that to her. I never said 'boo' about her drinking. That's why we stayed friends for so long.

Me: And that's why she gave you the Hawaii bracelet?

DS: [looks me straight in the eyes] Like I said, we were friends.

Me: My journalistic instincts are telling me that the bracelet may be more significant that it appears in Benny's book.

DS: It meant something to Bea. It was a kind of talisman.

Me: But it lacked the magical power to change her life.

DS: Maybe, but it was still important to her.

Me: But then she gave it to you. How long did you have it before you gave it to Benny at the funeral?

DS: Don't know. Seven, eight years maybe.

Me: And why do you think she gave it to you?

DS: I guess she realized she wasn't going to make it to Hawaii after all.

Me: Seven or eight years ago? Wasn't that about the time that Bea married Jack?

DS: Yes, I think it was.

Me: [speaking more softly] Mr. Serge, you know it was, don't you? Because that's when your affair with Bea ended. You gave her the bracelet. Maybe you found it together at a garage sale, maybe you planned to go there together. But then she gave you back the bracelet because she knew that she would never be going there with you. She would never be going anywhere with you, because she was marrying Jack. Isn't that right?

DS: [Squinting his eyes, he grimaced, but not painfully–as if he were looking far off, trying to see something that may or may not have been there. For a moment, I thought he might weep, but it passed, leaving a calm sadness in its wake.] Your journalistic instincts are good. Bea and I were lovers. For a while. Not a long while though. Six months and a few days.

Me: Your affair ended when Bea married Jack?

DS: No, it ended much before Jack. Bea said we were too good of friends to be lovers. Never made any sense to me, but that's what she wanted.

Me: But you still loved her?

DS: Till the very end. But there was nothing I could do except stay as close to her as our friendship would allow. My love was like one of those Jack pines growing in the rocks, all twisted and stunted because of poor growing conditions.

Me: Yet standing anyway, despite it all, against all odds.

DS: Yes, standing anyway.

What Happened When Ray Asked If He Could Stay on at the House and How Ray Met Rosie and Then We Both Met Reverend Grainger

Mr. Fairfux says things are moving along nicely and I should just keep going the way Im going so I guess thats what Ill do. When Ray asked me if he could stay on at the house it was a real shocker cause I guess I never thought me and Ray would ever be living under the same roof again. I knew Ray was a changed man but maybe deep down I was a bit afraid Ray would turn back into the old Ray I knew as a boy and Id have to suffer his bullying and his ass-pancakes and the rest of it as a grownup too. But like I said before I always thought of Ray and me as real brothers and I guess it meant I couldnt turn him away when he needed me so I gave him the spare room upstairs cause it was far away from my trains in the basement and I remembered how Ray felt about my trains. I mean I remembered Ray didnt like my trains mostly and thats why he stepped on my American Flyer locomotive but the truth was I didnt know why he didnt like them. It was kinda like the way Truck didnt like old Mrs. Crumley and her old dog Gus. I guess some people can just not like things without having a real good reason for not liking them or maybe there is a reason but they dont know it or they do know it but its something that makes them feel foolish or ashamed or something so they cant bring themselves to say it. I guess Ray was maybe ashamed that Jack never bought him nothing in his life mostly but dad bought me my first train set a few months before he set out for the Rockies in Canada to live like a black bear. I guess Ray hated my trains but he was ashamed to admit why he hated them and even though it was a long time ago I still thought it would be best if I kept Ray as far away from them as possible. Phil was dead set against the whole idea and he told me so. Hes using you Benny he said. Cant you see that? I said I couldnt and he said Benny youre too fuckin nice for your own good. Maybe I said. But hes my brother. Stepbrother said Phil. Not the same Benny. Not the same. I guess Phil was getting mad cause he picked up the broom and starting sweeping the new driveway real hard. Something bads gonna happen he said. Rays changed I said. He found the Lord I said and I knew it sounded stupid even as soon as I said it. The Lord? The Lord? said Phil raising his voice high but not really meaning them to be questions at all. Fuck the Lord Benny he said. Fuck the Lord! I guess it was right about then Ray showed up cause I heard the screen door slam behind me. Phil said Ray. What Ray said Phil. Phil Ill have to ask you not to take the Lords name in vain in my presence said Ray. It wasnt in vain said Phil cause I said it to offend you so that makes it not in vain at all. In fact that makes it purposeful is what it really makes it. I guess I knew I needed to jump in here somewhere but I wasnt exactly sure where or even how to for that matter but it turned out I didnt need to after all cause Ray turned the other cheek or at least thats what he told me later and he walked back into the house. Anyway after that Phil never come around as much as he used to and even when he did he pretty much stayed outside in the flowerbeds where I guess he felt most comfortable.

A few days after Ray moved in I had my first wet dream but it wasnt like it sounds cause I mean it wasnt like Ray had anything to do with my having the wet dream and it wasnt a real wet dream anyway. I mean it wasnt the kinda wet dream when youre a boy and you have a sexy dream about your favorite aunt and you wake up all wet from shooting in your sleep. I had them kinda wet dreams before like most other boys. I guess I had my first wet dream like that when

I was eleven and I panicked mostly cause I didnt know

what happened. Ray told me it meant I was very sick and my

little schnitzel was gonna fall off so for a week or so

after that I prepared myself to live like a girl for the

rest of my life by peeing sitting down and Ray thought it

was real funny when he saw me doing it. Anyway the dream

I had wasnt that kinda wet dream. I dreamed of Rosie and

when I woke up my undershirt was soaked with man-milk. I

mean I knew I could make my man-boobs shoot man-milk

just by thinking about Rosie but I never knew I could do

it in my dreams when I wasnt even trying to do nothing at

all. I got out of bed and walked to the bathroom to clean

up and Ray saw me all wet and sticky with man-milk and he

asked me what happened so I told him cause I thought he

was gonna find out sooner or later anyway. He looked at

me like the way you look at a big bug on the sidewalk real

careful cause youre not sure if its dead of if its just

sitting there or something. You mean your boobs give

milk? said Ray. And its this black lady of the night that

makes em do it? he said. I guess I pretty much laughed out

loud when Ray said lady of the night cause it sounded

like something Phil would make a joke about and it didnt

sound like Ray at all. The old Ray woulda said something

like scratch-snatch or pay-poon or slot-slut or something like that so I guess I knew then Ray really did change and it was all cause he found the Lord or the Lord found him I guess. I told him Rosie wasnt a lady of the night no more although I wasnt really sure it was true. I mean I didnt think Rosie was seeing other johns after I made her my chili con carne waffles but I guess she couldve been seeing other johns without me knowing about it and I guess it was her right to do it if she wanted to. So when do I get to meet the special lady? asked Ray. Why dont you bring her around tonight he said. The truth was I never really thought about bringing Rosie to the house cause I was kinda worried about what Phil might say to her but now Phil wasnt around mostly so I guess there wasnt no good reason not to no more. But maybe there was another reason I didnt bring Rosie around and by that I mean I felt guilty bringing another woman into Sams home. But I guess me and Phils trip to Sherm and Ellens pretty much changed that cause after I saw Sam and Beckys urns sitting there so sad on the mantle it hit me real hard they were gone. She was gone my Sam. She disappeared from my life and she wasnt coming back no matter what I did or didnt do. So what do you say? said Ray. Reverend Graingers coming around tonight. You can both meet the man that changed my life. Reverend Grainger is coming here tonight? I said. Yeah said Ray. I told you about it yesterday, remember? Its part of my parole stipulations. No I dont remember that I said. Oh said Ray. Well I told you all right. Trust me I did. Right then I guess I wished Phil was there cause I knew Phil would say something to Ray that I couldnt say myself. I mean I didnt mind the reverend coming to visit or nothing like that but I wasnt sure if I needed to read the Bible or something before he came. I guess I just thought Ray shouldve told me real clear Reverend Grainger was coming. Mr. Fairfux says I was feeling inconvenienced by the visit and I looked it up but I guess that dont sound quite right this time cause I think I was feeling more scared than anything. I mean I saw what the reverend did to Ray and I thought it was good but I also thought it was kinda a miracle and that Reverend Grainger wasnt like Father Owens at all cause he didnt just say prayers and talk lots about God and heaven and sin and hell but he seemed to do real stuff that wasnt just talking. I guess what Im saying is I thought he might change me too even though I wasnt real sure I needed changing. So I said to Ray Is he gonna make me find Christ? Ray kinda snorted like a horse with its nose buried in hay and said Benny he aint gonna make you do anything you dont wanna do. Okay? Okay I said but I thought maybe I should read a few verses of the Bible just in case.

I had to convince Rosie to come to the house but I could tell she really wanted to come and maybe she was even flattered some by me asking her. I thought she might be nervous some too on accounta Reverend Grainger being a reverend and her being a whore and all or maybe an ex-whore. I still wasnt sure but she said she was brought up real religious and she was no stranger to reverends and other men of God being around so we drove to the house in the Bel Air and I parked in the driveway for the first time since Sam disappeared. Mr Fairfux says it was a small but significant victory for me and I guess it pretty much was cause I sat there for a minute with my wrists resting on the steering wheel and my hands kinda hanging there and I sighed real loud I guess cause Rosie asked me if everything was alright and I said Yeah everything is great. Anyway we got there a bit early and I had the ginger ale that Ray asked me to pick up and when we got

inside it was pretty plain to see that Ray cleaned the
house real good when I was gone. The floor was vacuumed
and the coffee table looked like an ice rink and the pillows
on the sofa were turned so all the stains were pointing in
and not out. Right about this time Ray came out of the
kitchen with a bowl of cheez doodles and a bag of mini mars
bars. He looked real happy to see us and he set down the
snacks and gave Rosie a hug before I even got a chance to
properly introduce them. I guess Rosie didnt mind mostly
cause she laughed kinda high and hugged him right back.
Reverend Grainger showed up pretty much right after
that and like I said I was scared mostly to see him but I
guess I was excited too to meet the man who helped Ray find
the Lord. So I guess it was kinda a shocker when I saw him
and he was short and skinny and real white and when I say
he was real white I mean he was white all over. His long
hair and beard and skin and eyes were all the same white
color. Mr. Fairfux says he must have been an albino and
that sounds about right although I dont recall ever seeing
an albino before except for the rat named Russo in our
high school lab before I dropped out so I dont really
know if he was a real albino or not. Anyway like I said it
was a real shocker but part of me was angry some too cause

I thought Ray should tell me before Reverend Grainger
came that he looked the way he did so I wouldnt be shocked
and maybe not embarrass both me and the reverend. I guess
Rosie wasnt as shocked as me cause she took the reverends
hand and shook it real polite and said she was real happy
to meet him. Nice to meet you too little lady he said and I
thought he had an accent but I didnt know where from.
When he turned to me I kind froze up like I was a faucet in
the middle of a Wisconsin winter or something and I
couldnt get any words to come out that didnt sound like
squawks and garble or something. Ray said something
about my being nervous and Reverend Grainger put his
hand on my shoulder and said there was nothing to worry
about cause Jesus wants me to be happy and being happy
means being saved. Oh I said cause I didnt know what else
to say and Rosie squoze my hand real tight like everything
was alright. I guess it hit me right about then that Ray
asked the reverend around cause he wanted me to find the
Lord too and not really cause he was just trying to be
hospitable to Reverend Grainger and the truth was I
wasnt sure if I should be angry about that or not but I
finally decided not cause I guess Ray was just trying to
help me change and be happy like he was now. We all sat

down after the introductions and Ray poured a round of
ginger ale and I pecked nervously at the cheez doodles
and I have to say that it was hard not to notice the
reverend poured his drink down the front of his cream
colored suit a time or two and I figured maybe he was
blind some just like the way Russo the rat was blind some
and used to bump the walls of the glass cage with his pink
nose all the time. Anyway it wasnt long before Reverend
Grainger started talking about how me and Rosie could
find the Lord Jesus Christ the same as Ray did and the
same as all the other convicts did. Rosie said she already
gave herself to Jesus when she was a young girl and
Reverend Grainger said hallelujah and Ray said amen and
raised the Bible that he put down the back of his pants
the first six months of his sentence to protect him from
the bum bandits. But I let my faith lapse these past ten
years said Rosie and the reverend said Jesus loves a
sinner and Ray said Amen again and raised his Bible and
burped some from the ginger ale onto his chin. It was right
about then that Reverend Graingers white and pink eyes
settled on me and I guess he was waiting for me to say
something about Christ the Lord and all I could think of
was the Jehovahs Witness pamphlet from when I was a boy

so I said Jesus looked kinda like a movie star or at least a TV star. You know I said real handsome and the reverend said hallelujah and Ray said amen and raised his Bible and Rosie snickered some. Jesus is whatever you want him to be Benny said Reverend Grainger. Hes a movie star and a ditch digger and a politician and a car salesman and a surgeon and a dishwasher and a physicist and a pilot and a king. It dont matter said the reverend cause what he really is under all them things is a savior. Your savior Benny. Praise the Lord said Ray real loud and hallelujah said Rosie kinda loud. Then they were all looking at me so I said amen pretty soft and I have to say that it felt pretty good to say it so I said it a little louder. Amen said I. Amen said the reverend. Hallelujah said Ray. Praise the Lord said Rosie. Amen I said real loud this time like the way you yell when youre trying to yell overtop of some loud lawnmower or something.

I guess the evening went pretty much as planned or at least pretty much the way Ray and Reverend Grainger planned it so they were probably feeling pretty good. And me and Rosie were both feeling pretty good too about our Savior Jesus Christ so we said wed come to a revival

meeting next Sunday which I guess was the reverends
specialty or something at least thats what Ray said and I
guess the reverend traveled around the country in the
summertime helping people to find Christ the Lord. When
Reverend Grainger left I walked out onto the front porch
and I guess I was half expecting to see Phil in the rose
bushes there but he wasnt. I watched the reverend chug
away on a custom three wheel Harley Davidson motorcycle and
I wondered if he was nervous about driving since he was
pretty much blind and all so I asked Ray about it. The
good reverend fears nothing said Ray for the Lord is with
him always. Oh I said. Amen then I guess.

August 14

Made a call to Sylvester (aka Sylvia outside of 9 to 5) to find out where Gavin was. S. had a small part in Gavin's play and was also our neighbor in 5B. Said he hadn't seen Gavin since the last show. Asked if I'd heard the news about it being canceled and I said yes. Told him I hadn't heard from Gavin since then. Gave him my phone number at the Pinewood Lodge and asked him to call if he saw or heard from Gavin. Asked him to read the number back to me and he got defensive so I let him go with a terse good-bye.

August 14 (Later)

Drove my rental car down to the Holy Cross Church. It was the biggest building in this town of a couple thousand. And the only church. Dundee could've been my own hometown in rural Ohio. When I drove down the streets it was like I was driving down the street in the back of our old Plymouth Valiant wagon. Even the people I saw on the street I thought I recognized. The Holy Cross Church was a gothic cathedral-like stone building with a massive vault and two horizontally placed rose windows. The two towers and three spires at the front of the building made for an impressive façade.

Hadn't stepped in a church since I was a kid and hesitated slightly at the door. The vaulted ceiling was even more impressive from the inside. Shuffling down the aisle, I noted the organ pipes, and recalled how Truck had defecated in one of them.

Memories of a semi-lecherous priest from my own youth still haunted me and I fought the urge to turn around and leave. Stayed till mid-teens but finally left the church for good at sixteen. Truth was I wanted Father Owens to be flawed—not a monster—just clearly flawed. Somehow that would make me feel better. But he wasn't. Or at least he didn't seem that way. He was not what you'd call pleasant but he was accommodating enough. We settled into an office and he made herbal tea.

Interview Transcript: Father Alexander Owens

Me: Thank you for seeing me today, Father.

FO: That I don't know. I do know that it burnt to the ground. Most people around here believe it was Terry . . . Truck trying to get his father's attention.

Me: So Truck burned down the house.

FO: [no response]

Me: Okay then, back to the funeral. How did Benny seem to you then?

FO: Older. [smiling sheepishly at his attempt at humor] I didn't get a chance to speak with him alone, but he seemed content. Maybe even happy.

Me: So it is possible to achieve happiness in this life without the church?

FO: Of course, yes. But this life is fleeting. It's the next life that one needs to be concerned about.

What Happened When I Met Phil in the Park for Hoops and then Later I Went to Work and Talked to Rudy about God

The next morning I found Phil in Big Boys eating breakfast alone. I have to say that I was surprised and I guess hurt some that he never asked me to come along like the way he always used to. The truth was Phil and I drifted apart some after I started seeing Rosie and I guess Rays moving in was pretty much the final straw or final something anyway cause maybe we both said too many things that we shouldnta said. It was like a sea of words just kinda washed up between us or something and pretty soon we were so far apart we couldnt hardly see each other no more. Mr. Fairfux thinks thats a real nice waya putting it but Im no poet or nothing and thats just the way it seemed to me. Anyway I sat down and we ate together and Phil was quiet for a long time so I said the roses were dying and he said Winter is coming on and thats what roses do. I suppose so I said and I stuffed a piece of omelet in my mouth.

We went to the park to play hoops and I have to say it was pretty hard to jump or move around much cause the Big Boys breakfast was sitting in my belly like the way a brick sits in a gunny sack and I was worried some that I might have an accident like the time when Truck sharted in P.E. class and chased everyone around so he could sit on someones head and make them smell the death soup. I guess it was real lucky for me and for everyone else too that Mr. Novak saw what was going on and blew the whistle before Truck caught hold of anyone. The truth was I smelled the soup once before and I wasnt in no hurry to do it again anytime real soon. Anyway I wasnt doing real well on the basketball court today but it was good being around Phil again and hearing him talk about people and things the way he always did. He said something about turning political cause he was emceeing a fundraiser for the mayor and the mayor was trying to raise money so he could be mayor some more I guess. Fuckin dork said Phil. The only reason Im doing it is cause it may have a positive impact on my career. I guess I knew what he meant mostly about a positive impact cause I guess you could say that mean black dog that took my money satchel had a positive impact on my career cause I never woulda got fired from West Coast Vending and never woulda moved to the city and Phil never woulda found me my security guard job if not for that dog. Yeah positive impact I said and Phil grinned and passed me the ball. I have to say that I was surprised some that Phil never mentioned nothing about Rosie or Ray and I guess you could say it was kinda a shocker. So I told him about me and Rosie going to a revival meeting next Sunday and he laughed like I just said something real funny and I have to admit it sounded kinda funny to me too. The truth was I was expecting Phil to say something more than he did but what he said was pretty much nothing. I guess maybe I wanted him to say something more cause I wanted to know what he thought about me going to a revival meeting mostly but he didnt say nothing and that was the real shocker cause I knew what Phil thought about preachers and priests and religious types cause I heard him talk about them lots before on the radio. Just to make sure I said it again but Phil didnt say nothing again. When I left him later I felt kinda funny and not funny funny like haha funny but funny like the way you feel when you know someone you know good lied to you and you know they know they lied too but neither of you say nothing about it cause you think its just easier that way. Thats the way I felt when I said goodbye to Phil and walked back to the Bel Air alone.

I saw Rudy back on cleanup when I got to work and he looked lots better than the last time I saw him but I could still tell that he was sniffing floor wax again or something cause he always moved his head from side to side like he was following a fly buzzing around the room or something. When I saw Rudy doing that I always thought of Shane Tandy and how he did the same thing and never looked at you when he was talking to you and there were always white beads of spit in the corners of his mouth too. Truck said Shane Tandy was a stupid retard that was so stupid he had to wear a diaper cause he couldnt wipe his own arse. I mean thats what Truck said but I thought Truck probably shouldnt say nothing about it cause Truck was always doing the death soup thing in his shorts so he probably coulda used a diaper too sometimes. Truck used to kick Shane in the rear end every time Shane would pass by delivering groceries for Mr. Clarkes store. Mr. Clarke was real nice to Shane and I guess Truck couldnt ever figure out why and so he never liked Shane at all and I guess I never liked it much when Truck kicked Shane and called him Tandy the Tard but I didnt say nothing about it to Truck. Anyway Rudy wanted to thank me proper for

saving his life so he said we should go for a beer at
Orions Belt My Ass and I said okay and we crossed the
street and took two stools at the bar like the way we used
to. The truth was Id never gone there since I started
seeing Rosie kinda serious but I thought I might like to
go tonight partly cause there was a part of me that
wondered if Rosie never went there no more neither. I mean
I felt guilty some about wondering it but like I said I
still didnt know for sure one way or the other if Rosie
was really quit. I have to say that my heart kinda
hiccupped in my chest mostly when I saw a black girl in
the booth where Rosie was before with the fireman or the
policeman or the soldier or whatever he was. And I was
real relieved when it turned out the black girl wasnt
Rosie at all so I took a big gulp of beer and told Rudy me
and Rosie were going to a revival meeting next Sunday.
Rudy laughed real loud like the way Phil laughed and
said God is for chumps. Like I said I didnt know nothing
about Rudys past but I guess it was pretty much clear
Rudy had some kinda problem with God before so I asked
him straight out. Nothing specific said Rudy. I was
raised a run-of-the-mill church-going type said he.
When things went bad for me and sure as shit they always

seemed to the preacher kept promising me riches in heaven but I guess I got tired of waiting. The way I see it said Rudy is they just keep promising you this and that knowing they never have to make good on it. Fuck em I say said he. Oh said I like I was surprised but I really wasnt cause I guess I figured anyone who huffed the way Rudy huffed had to have something in his past that didnt sit right with them. But Im not saying anything about you and what youre doing said Rudy like he right then figured he said something he shouldnta. Im not sure what Im doing I said. Sounds like you got some interest in God and this preacher. Whats his name? Reverend Grainger I said. Yeah right said he. Sounds like this reverends maybe got his hooks into you. No I said. Its not like that. Whats it like said Rudy. I dont know for sure but its not like that. I guess hes got a gift or something I said. A gift for changing people. Rudy stopped and lit a cigarette and sat there real quiet like he was thinking about what I just said. There aint no gifts Benny he finally said. Theres just what people do and what people dont do and what people get away with and what people dont get away with. He grunted and said sounds like your Reverend Goodguys maybe got away with a lot in his lifetime. I guess I didnt

know what to say and so I didnt say nothing. I mean I wanted
to say that the reverend didnt seem to me like a guy who
was trying to get away with nothing but then I thought I
wouldnt know what a guy like that looked like anyway
even if I saw him. Dont get me wrong Benny said he. Were
all trying to get away with something. Its just that some
people have better luck at it than others. What are you
trying to get away with I asked. Rudy picked up his tequila
and shot it back. Me my man Benny he said. Just staying
breathing is what Im trying to get away with. So far so
good I said. Yep said he. So far so good.

What Happened When Me and Rosie Went to the Reverend Graingers Revival Meeting

I dressed pretty much like I always dressed cause I didnt really have any Sunday best clothes or nothing like that. The truth was Rosie cut holes around the nipples of all my shirts so I had to wear the brown tweed jacket that Phil gave me when he started getting fat after Steph left him. Still I have to say I felt foolish some when I saw Ray in his black suit and pink shirt and thin leather tie. I asked him about the tie and he said a con with a crush on him gave him the tie cause he hoped it might make Ray more open to a jailhouse relationship but it didnt at least Ray said it didnt and I guess I got no real reason to doubt him. I decided today to start wearing moms Hawaii bracelet she bought from a garage sale or something and she wore all the time until she gave up and gave it to Didier and Didier gave it to me at the funeral. I dont know for sure why I wanted to wear it but I did. Mr. Fairfux thinks it marked a new beginning for me cause I was about to enter a new phase of my life he says. Like I said I dont know for sure but I guess it could be something like that cause I was changing lots of things in my life right then and it seemed my old life with Sam was getting pretty far away in the

rearview mirror I guess you could say. Anyway I drove

the Bel Air and Ray sat in the passengers seat until we

got to Rosies place and then he slid over the seat into the

back. Rosie came out in a pink summer dress and I guess

that pretty much made sense since it was summer and all

and her nails were pink mostly and her lips were pink too.

I guess I wasnt the only one that thought she looked good

cause Ray whistled real soft from the backseat and Rosie

shushed him and leaned across the seat to peck me on the

cheek. I have to say it felt real good and I caught Ray

looking from the backseat and he looked like the time our

teenage cousin Trisha was visiting in the summer when

Ray was fourteen and I was eleven and she said she

started taking the pill a couple months before and I

didnt know what pill she meant but I could tell Ray did

cause all of a sudden he looked kinda scared and hopeful

too. Anyway we got to the meeting and it was a bit of a

shocker cause there was no church at all but just a big

tent and Ray said that Reverend Grainger had a church a

few years back somewhere in the Midwest but he gave it up

cause he liked taking Gods word on the road. It makes him

feel like a true disciple of the Lord said Ray. Oh I said

cause I didnt know that churches could move from town to town like a traveling show or something. Thats the way Jesus did it said Ray. Jesus had a tent I asked. Of course he had a tent Benny said Ray. He lived in the desert and people in deserts always have tents. Rosie grunted like she wasnt too sure about Jesus having in a tent in the desert but I thought it seemed about right so I didnt say nothing more about it. I parked the Bel Air in a dusty field and we went into the tent and sat down on metal chairs near the front. There was an old piano like the kind in our high school band room that everyone carved their initials in and an old man that looked like maybe he was Reverend Graingers dad was playing it real loud and he looked like he was enjoying it lots too. The tent filled up real fast and pretty soon Reverend Grainger walked up to the front of the stage wearing a long white robe and a big wooden cross hung around his neck and he looked like an angel ready to float away or something except the only thing holding down was the big cross. I guess I jerked in my seat some when he started talking cause I wasnt expecting it to be so sudden and so loud and his eyes were pinker than before and he wasnt looking at nothing or at least thats the way it seemed to me. The reverend said Jesus was coming back and vengeance was gonna be his on that great and terrible day and only people who repented and gave themselves to Jesus would not be consumed by the fires of hell. I guess I kinda knew there was fire in hell but I didnt know that it was the kinda fire thats all over the place mostly and never goes out. I guess I always thought it was a bonfire or something in Hell like the kind thats got a couple of railway ties in it so it gets real hot and high and scorches the trees all around and it smells like diesel fuel so you get a real bad headache just sitting there staring at it. Anyway Ray and all the others jumped out of their seats and kept yelling out Amen and Hallelujah and Praise the Lord and all that so I had a hard time making heads or tails out of what the reverend was saying but the truth was I already knew I was ready to accept Jesus into my life so it didnt much matter. I guess I knew right after talking to the reverend at the house mostly but I thought about it some that night and the next day some too just to make sure. I even tried to talk to God about it but then I thought talking to God was kinda stupid cause of course God is gonna tell me to accept Jesus into my life cause Jesus pretty much works for God anyway. So like I said I already knew what I was gonna do when I got to Reverend Graingers revival meeting. When the reverend finished his sermon the old man at the piano began to play again real loud a kinda happy sounding song and Reverend Grainger invited me up to the front of the tent to accept Jesus into my life but I was nervous about it now so I grabbed Rosies hand and she followed me up even though she had already accepted Jesus into her life a long time ago. The reverend said do you accept the Lord Jesus Christ into your life right now? He looked real serious and his long white hair was full of static or something cause it was kinda sticking up and his pink eyes were big and dry and so I said yes I do accept him I do. The reverend stepped forward and put his hand on my head and I felt a big shock like the time I stuck Jacks Camaro keys into the wall socket cause it snapped real loud and I felt my knees go kinda weak and rubbery and I guess I fell backwards. The next thing I knew Rosie was holding me up and breathing heavy on my neck saying hallelujah and kinda licking my neck and flicking my nipples with her pink nails under Phils jacket and right about then the jacket fell open and my man-boobs shot man milk like two squirt guns or something right into the eyes of Reverend

Grainger. The reverend screamed like the way your aunt screams when she finds out your teenage cousin is pregnant but then he stopped and rubbed his eyes and he looked at me real clear and shouted hallelujah and the old man at the piano pretty much went crazy banging on the keys. I can see shouted the reverend. I can see perfectly and then he looked down at my two nipples dripping on my shirt and he smiled real big. Praise the Lord he shouted real loud this time and he turned me around to the crowd and I could feel a breeze tickle the nipples of my man-boobs and he said brothers and sisters its a miracle and they all shouted amen back at him. I looked out at the rows and the black and white faces and I guess it was right about then I saw a familiar one from when I was a boy. There in the back row with his sunglasses on and his hair shiny and hard was Truck.

August 17

Been pretty successful so far at getting people to talk to me. Only person who refused was Phil. Made a half-hearted attempt to track down his ex-wife Stephanie but gave up when the trail ran cold in San Francisco. Phil was the one I wanted anyway. Felt Benny's story was incomplete without Phil's take on things. Thought about trying to ambush him at work but couldn't get into the building. Sat outside (again) in my rented Honda Accord and listened to his show. Then followed him when he came out. Just as I'd hoped, he headed straight for Big Boy's. Waited for him to sit, order, get his meal. Then went inside and sat down in his booth. He must've remembered me showing up unannounced at his house a while ago.

Interview Transcript: Philip Wilkes

PW: Should of known you wouldn't give up so easily. [slurps at black coffee then scoops hash browns into his mouth]

Me: An 18-wheeler omelet?

PW: Only thing on the menu worth having.

Me: So Benny was right, then.

PW: About that.

Me: You don't think he was right about anything else?

PW: Don't know what he said about anything else. But in case you haven't noticed, Benny isn't all there all the time. He doesn't see things the way they really happen.

Me: Or maybe he does see things the way they really happen and the rest of us don't.

PW: Whatever you say, boss.

[A young blond waitress who ages twenty years as she strolls up the aisle toward us asks if I want anything; I order coffee and pie with a dollop of whipped cream.]

Me: What happened with you and Benny? What was at the root of your falling out?

PW: Falling out? [grunts] What does Benny say.

Me: He doesn't really. At least, not definitively. He seems to suggest, in his own way, that it had something to do with Rosie and Ray.

PW: He said that?

Me: More or less.

PW: Maybe he's not as thick as I thought.

Me: So he's right, then. You didn't approve of Rosie and you didn't like Ray.

PW: No, I didn't like Ray He's a freeloading opportunistic asshole. And I didn't approve of Rosie? She was a whore. What's to approve of? [setting down his fork and dabbing at his mouth with a ketchup-stained napkin] Look, I didn't care that Benny was seeing a whore. I'm no stranger to wh–[stops abruptly, peers at me menacingly, then continues slowly]. It wasn't that she was a working girl. It was the weird shit they were doing together. Or didn't he mention that?

Me: The suckling? Most of his manuscript is about their suckling.

PW: Then what do you want me for? You've got the story.

Me: I want to know more about Benny. About how he and your sister met. About your first meeting. All of those things.

PW: Why don't you ask Benny? He was there, too. [looks up with his eyes, challenging yet somehow lonely or maybe just sad]

Me: When you're in my line of work, a ghost-writer-slash-book-doctor, you quickly learn that all memoirs are one-dimensional. They are just one version of the whole story. And the more versions you get, the closer you are the whole story. I'm not here to say that Benny's version or your version is right or wrong, truth or lies. I simply want to get a better understanding of the whole story.

PW: I tell you what . . . I'll answer your questions as long as I don't have to listen to another line of bullshit like that. Deal?

Me: [snickering, shaking my head] Deal.

PW: So what do you want to know?

Me: Tell me about the first time you met Benny.

PW: I first met Benny at the hospital. Sam had just graduated and started working at a hospital just up the road in Newberg. But she didn't have her driver's license, so I picked her up after my show when she had night shifts. One night Benny just sort of showed up there. I could tell Sam was a little embarrassed and surprised at seeing him there. But she introduced us and he seemed okay, although I could tell right away that he was a bit slow. He was still working for that vending machine company and he wanted to give her a ride home in the van. But I didn't like the idea, so I made her come home with me. But then the same thing happened the next night and the night after that. I could tell Sam wanted to go with him, so I finally let him give her a ride home.

Me: Why do you think Sam saw in Benny? I mean, why do you think she was attracted to him?

PW: Well, Sam was beautiful in her own way . . . but not in any conventional way. She was never popular, never played on any teams or joined any clubs. Let's just say she'd never been special in any way. Benny made her feel special. So I guess that's what she liked about him.

Me: Like the old saying goes, "There's a lid for every pot."

PW: Yeah, something like that.

Me: So then, after Samantha died, it must have bothered you to see Benny dating someone like Rosie. Someone who was not at all like your sister.

PW: Well, yeah, but look, you're not going to turn this back onto me, and in your pinko, P.C., liberal way make it seem like I was the one with the problem. I didn't have a problem with Benny moving on and trying to be happy. I mean, shit, I was trying to do the same myself. I was more worried about where things were going to end up with all that suckling bullshit. I figured that Benny would find himself in a worse place. And I was right, wasn't I?

Me: I honestly don't know. Who's to say he's worse off now than before? He has hope, something he hasn't had since Samantha died. And he was happy for a time, at least it seems that way.

PW: That's all whitewash bullshit. You can spin it however you want in that book of his, but the truth is he would've been better off if he'd never met the whore.

Me: You mean he'd be better off if he were still sad and alone . . . just like you.

PW: [no answer, just a disapproving look, ending with an abrupt exit]

What Happened With Rosie and Me after I Accepted Jesus
as My Lord and Savior and We Went Back to Her Place
and then to My Place and Later to a Church Picnic

Mr. Fairfux says I shouldnt say too much about seeing
Truck again right now cause there will be more on that
later and I need to stick with the story about me and
Rosie so Ill just say that it was awkward some at first
seeing Truck. I said hello and we shook hands and I
introduced Rosie and I saw Truck look her over like the way
you look over your uncles souped-up Charger or something.
The truth was Truck didnt really seem changed to me in the
same way Ray seemed changed and I guess it made me wonder
if he really accepted Jesus as his Lord and Savior. He
told me he was working for Reverend Grainger now and I
asked what he was doing for the reverend and he said
bodyguard and I said oh cause I didnt know preachers
needed bodyguards like the way movie stars or something
did. Theres some real sickos out there Benny he said. Yeah
I guess I said but I didnt know what kinda sicko he meant
cause I couldnt think why any sicko at all would wanna do
anything to Reverend Grainger. I said Im a guard too. A
security guard but Truck didnt seem real interested in

my job so I said see you around I guess and he said yeah you

will Benny and that was that for the time being anyway.

Rosie didnt say nothing about Truck but I asked her about

him cause I guess I thought she knew men pretty good and

she said she knew his type. What type? I asked. Lonely and

selfish and cruel she said. Dont care about anyone. I said

that sounded about right at least it sounded about right

from what I remembered about Truck.

Me and Rosie went back to her apartment and I could tell

something was bothering her cause she kept on getting up

and moving things around for no good reason I could see.

So finally I asked her. Its just that I havent been working

lately she said. I sat real quiet and watched her pick up a

flower vase from the kitchen table and move it to the

mantel of a small gas fireplace with fake black logs that

looked kinda like they already melted a bit or something.

Youll probably think this is stupid but since you and I

have been together I just havent been able to bring myself

to turn any tricks. I guess I smiled cause she put her

hands on her hips and said What? What is it? Nothing I

said. No really. What is it? she said. Well I was wondering

about that I said the tricks. But I didnt wanna ask. Benny

she said and she sighed kinda sad and long. You dont think
I could give myself to another man after being with you
do you? I dont know I said. I guess not. Rosie sat down
again and dug her fingers into my hair some and said we
have something real special here Benny. Yeah I know it I
said. So whats bothering you then? I didnt wanna say
nothing she said. But now I think I have to. I guess I was
worried some or probably anxious like Mr. Fairfux would
say but I tried not to let on so I just listened and tried to
look real calm. I got an eviction notice this morning said
Rosie. Youre getting evicted? I asked kinda relieved
cause I guess I was pretty much expecting something lots
worse. Yes Benny she said. Im being evicted. When? I asked.
Soon she answered. I sat there for a minute kinda dumb I
guess cause I was happy it wasnt something real serious
but then I got a crazy idea and I dont mean crazy crazy
but more like exciting crazy. The truth was Rosie was
probably waiting for me to get the idea and finally say
it cause she sat there with her legs curled up under her
and she was looking at me like the way you look at someone
thats telling you a story you already heard before but
you think maybe you missed some important detail or
something and thats why theyre telling the story again.

Why dont you move into the house? I said. Your house? she said. Yeah my house I said. Oh Benny she said and Rosie wrapped her arms around my neck and she pulled me close like she was gonna whisper something in my ear but she kissed me instead and I guess thats just as good or maybe even better.

The next day me and Rosie filled up the Bel Air with her clothes and took them to the house. Ray didnt seem to care much about Rosie moving in but Phil did. I guess he came to the house to work in the roses again when I was at work and he met Rosie and he tried to act like it didnt matter but Rosie said she could tell it did. Rosie said she was sure Phil didnt like her so I said Phil dont really like nobody I know of. Then I told her what Phil did cause I thought it might help explain some about why Phil dont really like nobody and Rosie kinda gasped and said I thought I recognized that voice. Hes the one whos always phoning local celebrities and calling them fat she said. Yeah thats him I said. He only has one testicle I said but I wasnt sure why I said it except maybe I thought it might help explain some too why Phil acts like does. Right about then Ray walked into the room and I guess he

overheard us cause he said dont worry about Phil. Hes
what Revered Grainger calls a bitter apple cause one raw
bite is enough to make you sick to your stomach but if you
bake it just so in the piping-hot love of Christ it makes
for a fine apple pie. Rosie half snorted and half laughed
and said she liked the reverend. Thats good said Ray cause
he likes you too. In fact he wants to speak to you two about
something important. Really? said Rosie. Yep said Ray.
Theres a church picnic tomorrow night and Reverend
Grainger would like you two to be his guests of honor. I have
to say that I was real flattered cause I never remembered
being a guest of honor at anything except for maybe my
wedding but I wasnt sure that counted or not. So what do
you say? said Ray and Rosie looked at me and I looked at her
and she said sure and so did I. Alright then its settled
said Ray. Reverend Grainger will be happy to hear it said
Ray. I can assure you of that.

Me and Sam didnt look at many places before we bought
this house cause I guess we pretty much knew right away
that it was the right place for us. I liked the basement
and I promised to finish it and make it into a family
recreation room but I never did so it ended up just being a

bare cement room for my trains. Sam liked that the two bedrooms upstairs faced each other cause she said it would be perfect for baby Becky being so close. But I guess I already explained that never happened cause little Becky never came home from the hospital at all. Anyway it was kinda hard the first couple of nights when Rosie moved in cause I guess I never thought Id ever have another woman in mine and Sams bedroom. I liked to sleep with the door open like the way I imagined me and Sam woulda slept with little Becky across the hall but Rosie liked to sleep with the door closed and I guess that made sense cause Ray was in the bedroom downstairs and he might hear me and Rosie suckling at night before bed. After Officer Dalton got called to the fancy coffee coffee shop me and Rosie mostly quit suckling in public and did it all in private now but I guess there was the one time about a month or so after Rosie moved in and it pretty much ended me and Phil being brother-in-laws or at least I never saw him around the house after that. Anyway one day Rosie told me about a big meeting at a fancy hotel downtown and we thought wed go there and suckle in public one last time. I didnt know till we got there that it was a dinner for the mayor cause he was raising money for his next campaign I guess

so we bought two tickets and sat at a table near the front.
Me and Rosie ate roast beef and drank wine some and we
were both feeling pretty good when I saw Phil walk out
onto the stage of the ballroom with a mike in his hand and
I have to say that it was a real shocker. I mean it was a
shocker mostly cause Phil always used to make fun of the
mayor on his radio show and I knew Phil hated the mayor
cause he called him a donkey-dicked baboon when he wasnt
on the radio. I guess I looked surprised and he looked
surprised too when he saw me and Rosie sitting there.
Anyway pretty soon Rosie opened my jacket and started
flicking with my nipples the way I like it and then she
started licking them with her tongue and I guess by then
we were pretty much suckling full on right there. The
lights were down low mostly so no one seemed to notice at all
but Phil noticed cause I saw his jaw drop and his eyebrows
kinda squirm like caterpillars on a thin branch or
something when he saw us and I guess I knew right then
that Phil wouldnt be coming around no more. When me and
Rosie got back to the Bel Air I told her about Phil and
what he thought about the mayor and his saying the
mayor could have a positive impact on his career but it
was still a real shocker to see him there tonight. Rosie

said hes right Benny. About what? I said. Advancing his
career she said. Who knows what kinda opportunities
might come out of this for Phil? I guess youre right I
said although I pretty much never thought of Phil as
trying to advance nothing except a basketball on the
one-on-one courts at Stafford Park.

Reverend Grainger was waiting for me and Rosie to get to
the church picnic and I have to say I was nervous some to
see if the miracle my man-milk did last Sunday still worked
or not. I didnt have to wait long to find out cause the
reverend walked right over real confident and sure about
where he was going and not bumping into nothing and he
looked me straight in the eye and I could see his eyes
werent pink so much no more but were blue mostly and he
shook my hand real solid and said here you are Benny my
miracle maker. I mean I didnt know what to say to that and
when I thought I might just say thanks I saw Truck making
his way over to us. Hey Benny said Truck. I understand you
two know each other said Reverend Grainger. Yeah I said.
But that was a long time ago wasnt it Benny said Truck.
Yeah I guess it was I said. By the way great miracle last
week said Truck. That thing with your man-boobs is mind-

blowing I tell you. Thanks I said. Then the reverend led
us to a table right under an oak tree and we sat in the
shade and ate corn on the cobb and potato salad with lots
of onions and I thought about when Truck and I used to
say stupid stuff like Ooh la la! and Mon cherry at the
church socials in the basement of Holy Cross Church and I
guess I wondered if Truck remembered it too and I mightve
asked him but couldnt cause the reverend was telling
stories about being on the road with his revival meetings
and how the Lord and Savior had blessed him with an
abundance of followers. Me and Rosie listened mostly and
Truck just sat picking his teeth with the blade of a
miniature jackknife and I wondered if it was the same
jackknife Truck used to flatten Shane Tandys bicycle
tires every week just cause he thought Shane was a stupid
retard. Pretty soon a band with a banjo and fiddle player
started up and some of the crowd got up and danced. It was
still daylight so I thought they looked foolish mostly
out there dancing in the tall grass like they were drunk
on hillbilly gin or something. I guess I only ever saw
people dance at weddings but I dont know if you could
really call it dancing cause it always seemed to me more
like they were just shuffling their feet between drunken

tip-overs. Anyway Truck asked Rosie to join him for a dance in the grass and it was a real shocker cause I never thought of Truck as the dancing kind before but Rosie said okay and followed him away from the table and she started moving kinda slow and sexy and Truck did some dance that looked like maybe he should be wearing a kilt or something. I guess this was the opportunity Reverend Grainger was waiting for cause he leaned in on the table and cleared his throat like he was gonna say something serious like that way a policeman clears his throat just before he tells your mom that your brother was picked up for selling dope at school again. Benny he said I think you have a gift. A gift? I said. Yes a gift he said. But not just any gift a gift from God. Him saying it was a real shocker to me cause I never really thought of it like a gift from anyone specially God and I mean I wasnt brought up religious or nothing like that but I never remembered any story from the Bible about man-milk and it making miracles happen so I said so. Youre right about that Benny said the reverend. But these are different times and different times require different miracles. I guess I said. Do you think its coincidence that this happened to you now? he asked. I wasnt sure exactly what now he meant

so I guess I just kinda grunted. Do you think it is a
coincidence that you came to my meeting and healed my
eyes and blessed me with clear eyesight? I guess not I
said. Certainly not said the reverend. It is a sign from
God. A gift from God and a sign from God too? I said. Thats
right said he. A gift and a sign and also a spiritual
connection. We are connected spiritually you and I by the
miracle. Oh I said but I admit I didnt know what a spiritual
connection was so I thought Id ask Ray about it later. I
think God wants you and me to team up Benny he said. Team
up? I said. Yes, team up. I want you to join me on the road
said the reverend. But what would I do? I said. You would
squirt your miraculous man-milk all over the sick and
afflicted he said and heal them just like you did me. Oh I
said but I couldnt help thinking about what Officer
Dalton might say about doing something like that. I cant
do it without Rosie I said. Shes the one who makes it
happen. I have to say I felt guilty some for lying to the
reverend cause I knew I could make my man-boobs squirt
man-milk just by thinking about Rosie but I didnt wanna
go on the road without her. I guess I couldnt bear the
thought of leaving her behind. Youre sure thats what God

wants me to do? I said. Oh yes Benny said the reverend. I

am sure thats what God wants you to do.

August 22

Got a phone call from Sylvester. He was whispering like there was something wrong. Asked him why he was whispering. Said he didn't know except maybe it was because of what he had to tell me. Asked him what it was and he said he saw Gavin last night through the fisheye of his door. Just after midnight. "OK." I said. "And?"

"He was in the hall, grinding against an older gentleman."

I'd been steeling myself for news like this. Unfortunately, you're never ready for it because you don't know when it's coming so preparing yourself for it is a pointless endeavor. It always catches you off guard. The only thing I could think to ask was, "Who?"

Sylvester didn't know. Said he didn't get a clear look at him but he looked older and quite refined. Wondered if that meant I wasn't refined.

Thanked him absently and hung up the phone. Staring at nothing. Just staring. Until my limbs tingled prickly and numb and my back felt like red hot rebar. Don't know how long I sat there. An hour. Maybe two. Until finally I gave into the pull of deep, dreamless sleep

How I Got Ray a Job and Me and Rosie Went Out on the Road
with Reverend Grainger

I guess Ray didnt mind me going on the road mostly cause
he got the whole house to himself for a couple of months.
I got Ray a job working clean-up with Rudy so he had some
money now and he said he could pay me rent for staying at
the house but I told him it was okay and I didnt want him
to pay me rent but I wanted him to watch out for Rudy some
instead. He said he would and God could change anyone
even Rudy and I said that would be great if he could and I
meant it cause I thought if anyone needed changing it was
Rudy. I mean I guess it was kinda lucky I was there last
time Rudy ODd but I thought maybe I wouldnt be there one
of these times so if God could change him like the way Ray
was changed then it would save me lots of trouble and
maybe save Rudys life too.

I drove to Phils house before me and Rosie left with
Reverend Grainger but he wasnt there or he wasnt
answering the door. After me and Rosie suckled at the
mayors dinner that night I never saw him again and I
even went to Big Boys a few Saturday mornings but I

guess he found somewhere else to get an 18 Wheeler omelet. Before me and Phil started going for the 18 wheeler omelet Steph used to make Phil omelets at home Saturday mornings before she left him after he started acting all weird about losing one of his testicles. I guess Phil knew things werent going good when he started finding all kinds of things in his omelets that shouldnt be in omelets like corn and peanuts and anchovies and even a couple sticks of spearmint gum. One day he said to me I gotta get a goddamn omelet with some meat and cheese in it and thats pretty much when we started going to Big Boys real regular. Anyway me and Rosie drove out to the same place as the church picnic and there was a big white bus there that had REJOICE! written real big on the side of it and I thought about how the reverend had said rejoice real loud when I sprayed him with man-milk and suddenly he could see again like the way you wake up in the morning and scrape the sleep gunk out of your eyes before you can get them to focus right I guess. I mean I never saw nobody that happy before and it kinda made me happy too but also scared some cause I didnt know then that my man-milk had healing powers or nothing like that. A couple of two two-ton trucks were lined up behind the bus but they didnt have anything written on them except one of the back doors said if this truck is not being driven in a safe and courteous manner please call 111-HEAVEN and ask for your maker. Rosie thought it was pretty funny but I have to say it didnt make much sense to me but then I guess I was never one to get jokes much and especially ones about God and religion. Reverend Grainger got off the bus and came over to the Bel Air and said hello and asked if we were ready to go out and get some converts and I said I guess so yes. Then he invited us to ride with him in the bus and sing traveling songs but I said we would follow along behind in the Bel Air. Suit yourself he said and he got back on the bus. So me and Rosie followed the bus and two trucks about ninety miles to a small town near the border and we set up camp in a campground next to a river that was more rocks than water and I guess that would make it more a stream than river. I dont know why I was surprised some to see Truck step off the bus and walk over to us with a tent. Reverend Grainger says you should use this he said. Thanks I said. You need some help setting it up he said. No thanks I said and I felt my face redden some cause I guess Truck was remembering the time when me and him camped down by Cheaters Gulley and my tent looked like it was set up by a blind man cause it had poles poking out in all directions and in the moonlight it reminded me of a porcupine under a blanket or something. I set up the tent and me and Rosie joined the reverend and the others around the campfire. They were making cheese stuffed smokies on hot dog buns and it was okay with me except I could never get the smokie to stay in the bun right and the cheese inside burned my tongue real bad. Me and Rosie sat down and Reverend Grainger poured us some coffee and he said he was sorry there was nothing stronger but the body is a temple he said. Oh I said and I looked over at Truck cause I guess I knew Truck drank beer since he was nine years old and he smiled and drank his coffee real quiet.

The night was real clear and the stars were real bright and Rosie and me sat by the fire for a long time looking up and not saying nothing. Then we started to suckle and I guess I felt kinda like I did before when we were suckling in the movie theater cause I wanted to tell Rosie how I felt again but I couldnt same as before. I didnt feel as down about it this time like I did last time though cause I guess I figured Rosie already knew what I wanted to say anyway and when I thought about it thats how things

were with me and Sam too. I dont remember ever saying
much to Sam about feelings mostly or nothing else like
that but I guess she knew too. Sometimes Sam looked at me
like the way you look at your baseball glove you found in
the ditch after it fell off your handlebars and you
thought it was lost for good and I knew how she was
feeling without her saying a thing and I guess thats how
it was when I looked at her too. Im no philosopher or
nothing like that but I guess I know that words dont
really change much all by themselves and so they arent
missed so much when we dont say them but we just do them
instead. I hope Mr. Fairfux has a better way of saying
what I just tried to say but he says its good and he likes
it so I guess it stands as is then. Anyway like I said me
and Rosie suckled under the stars and my man-milk looked
like black blood or something running down her chin and
her eyes were closed mostly but sometimes she opened them
and they glowed some in the moonlight. I guess I was
harder than a railway tie in Alaskan permafrost like
Phil always used to say cause my man-thing was getting
ready to blow but I heard a sound in the bushes behind me
and Rosie that kinda distracted me I guess so I turned

around and I thought I saw Trucks red hair disappearing into the trees like a dying torch or something.

The next day I went to see Reverend Grainger in his bus cause he wanted to talk about the meeting tonight and Truck was there with his head under the bus hood but he didnt see me so I didnt say nothing but just got on the bus and sat down. The reverend wore army boots and cut off fatigues and a T-shirt that said Satan is for sissies and I have to say that it was a bit of a shocker. I guess he noticed me looking at his clothes so he said this is my work attire. Work? I said. Yes he said. You see Benny theres more to Gods work than simply preaching the good word. The tent has to be set up and the chairs and sound system and the piano have to be humped from the trucks to the tent. But youre blind I said. Was blind said the reverend. Thanks to you and your miraculous man-milk I can do all the things I couldnt do before. You see Benny all my life Ive been led around and taken care of. Im albino you know. Legally blind. I can see faint images but I cant see anything more than that. Or I couldnt I should say. Reverend Grainger closed up the Bible that was open in front of him on the table. What happened to make you an albino I said. Nothing happened Benny. I was born that way he said. God made you that way? I said. Well yes I believe he did. I believe my mamma birthed a white runt pup like me for a reason. Gods reason. Oh I said. Whats the reason? Reverend Grainger leaned in kinda close and said you Benny. God made me an albino cause he knew one day I would meet you and you would heal me and together we would do great things for the kingdom of God on earth. I have to say that it felt like my gut sprung a thousand leaks or something when the reverend said it and I guess I pretty much knew he was right like the way you know the rivers gonna freeze in winter and the hockeyll be better than last year cause of it. Like I said I was never raised churchy or nothing but I sure felt something kinda close to churchy when I heard the reverend say that. Reverend Grainger explained how things were gonna work in the meeting and he gave me a white robe that looked kinda like the robe I remember Jesus wore on the front of the Jehovahs Witnesses pamphlet except this robe had two quarter-size holes for my nipples. Just make sure to squirt em good he said and he laughed some like it was funny but not real funny. Okay I said and I took my

robe and got off the bus and I decided to say hello to
Truck this time but the bus hood was down and he was gone.

I was nervous some when it came time for the meeting.
After the tent was all set up I went down to the river that
was more like a stream and I washed my private areas real
good and put on the white robe that Reverend Grainger
gave me. Then me and Rosie watched from our tent and cars
pulled up and people got out and they were holding Bibles
real tight to their sides and chests and thats when we
heard the piano music coming from inside and I knew I was
supposed to go cause the reverend told me so earlier. I
took Rosies hand and we walked through the grass to the
meeting kinda slow and we went in and out of the cars and
I looked at Rosie in her white lace dress and I said You
look real good and she said Thank you Benny real shy like
she wasnt expecting it or something. I guess there was
about fifty people in all in the big tent and they were
sitting in their chairs kinda swaying to the piano music
of the same old piano player as before but now I knew him
as Will the piano player and some of them were clapping
their hands and singing along. The men wore suits with
bolero ties and pointed shoes and the women wore dresses

with matching hats and their hair was grey mostly but some was blonde and brown and piled high on their heads. Me and Rosie sat at the back like Reverend Grainger said to and waited and pretty soon the reverend came out and right then I thought he looked like Moses at the end of the movie that always made mom cry but I could never understand why. Reverend Grainger starting talking real loud and at first just a few people said praise the Lord and amen but pretty soon pretty much the whole crowd was saying it and some even got out of their seats. I have to say I didnt hear what the reverend said mostly cause I was real nervous about my part in the meeting and it was coming up real soon. Finally Reverend Grainger said something about a guest healer and I heard my name and next thing I knew Rosie was leading me to the front of the tent and I could feel all the eyes looking at me up and down and wondering what it was I was gonna do. Reverend Grainger said brothers and sisters in Christ I stand before you a man who was once blind but now can see cause of good brother Benjamin here who God has blessed with the healing balm of man-milk that can work miracles among the faithful. I guess I stood there for a while and the piano of Will the piano player jangled behind me some

slow and kinda sad song and pretty much everyone in the
tent sat and watched and waited until finally a lady
somewhere in the middle of the tent stood up and walked to
the front. I guess she was in her forties but it was hard
to tell cause she had lots of makeup on and she looked
real serious which always makes someone look older than
they are or at least thats what mom always used to say
and I guess she was pretty much right cause she looked
seventy ever since my dad left to live like a black bear in
the Rockies of Canada. I couldnt tell what was wrong with
her and I guess the reverend couldnt neither cause he said
and what is it that ails you dear sister and she looked at
him like she didnt hear him and I guess she didnt cause he
said it again and pretty soon it was clear she was deaf as
a rubber mallet. Reverend Grainger put a hand on my
shoulder and he said step forward dear sister that
brother Benjamin might anoint you with man-milk and
the dear sister stepped forward and put her ear next to
my chest. I have to say I was real nervous now and nothing
was coming out of my man-boobs so Rosie started flicking
my nipples up and down like the way she always did and
she nibbled on my ear so I could hear her breath in one ear
and the piano was loud in my other ear. Before I knew it

my man-thing jumped in my robe and pretty soon man-milk
was flowing like one of them peeing fountains right into
dear Sisters ear. I guess she was surprised some cause she
gave a little squeal and she stuck a finger in her ear and
jiggled it all around and then she smiled real big and the
makeup on her face looked like it might crack or something.
The reverend said dear sister and she said yes yes I can
hear you. Praise the Lord she said and Reverend Grainger
said praise the Lord and everyone in the tent said praise
the Lord too. And right then Rosie whispered praise the
Lord in my ear and my man-thing twitched and I doused
the dear sister again.

The next morning me and Rosie woke up to some hymn singing
outside the tent so we got up and joined the reverend and
the others for prayer and breakfast and everyone seemed
in a real good mood and they all smiled at me and said
Benny. Even Truck smiled and sat down and ate ham and
scrambled eggs with me and Rosie. You did good Benny he
said. Reverend Grainger is real happy with last night.
Thanks I said. Twenty converts in one night said Truck.
Thats a new record said Reverend Grainger and he sat
down on a log beside me. A record? I said. Yes indeed he

said. You brought twenty people to Christ the Lord last night Benny. Thats more than weve ever had in one night before. Then Reverend Grainger pulled some bills out of his pocket and handed them to me and said theres your cut Benny. Thanks I said and I guess maybe I looked guilty some or something cause the reverend said The Lord dont expect you to quit your job and work for free. You understand Benny? he said. Yeah I do I said.

August 30

Drove the thirty miles to Salem to visit Ray again. Gave him the batteries and cigarettes he likes. He immediately lit up. Recalled something B. wrote about Ray and his once newfound belief that the body is a temple, but decided not to waste time asking about something that he may or may not have said. Or more likely, something he'd probably just deny saying anyway.

Interview Transcript: Raymond Kaczka (Part Two)

Me: I'd like to pick up from where we left off last time. I was asking you about Benny's relationship with his mother. Can you tell me something about that?

RK: Not much to tell. She was drunk as a lord all the time, so Benny had to fend for himself . . . same as everyone else.

Me: You mean you and your father.

RK: [nods, pushing blasts of smoke from either nostril]

Me: In his manuscript, Benny writes about falling on a rusty nail and spending the night alone in the hospital. He said his mother never came in to see him. Do you recall that?

RK: Not specifically, no. But that sounds about right. She wasn't much good for any kind of responsible thing 'less you caught her first thing in the morning.

Me: Okay, lets change the topic to Reverend Grainger. Are you still in contact with him?

RK: [chuckling smugly] You're shittin', right?

Me: Not really, no.

RK: Nobody's been in touch with the Reverend. Last I heard, he was hiding out in San Fran somewhere. After everything that happened, I figure he won't be takin' his show on the road again anytime soon.

Me: But you believed in him once. You believed in his mission to bring people to Jesus.

RK: I woulda believed in the Devil himself if he'd promised to get me out of the pokey before my time was up.

Me: And why do you think he did that . . . got you out early?

RK: Needed recruits. Takes grunts to run a show like his. And cons are easy to control 'cause you just threaten to send 'em back inside.

Me: But you never worked for him.

RK: That's only because he met Benny. And he wasn't interested in me after that.

Me: Do you ever see Benny? Does he still come to visit?

RK: Not much. I saw him once last Christmas. That's about it.

Me: Do you ever think about Rosie? Were you sorry to hear what happened to her?

RK: Yeah, sure. Truth is I liked Rosie. She never deserved what happened to her.

Me: And Truck . . . did he deserve what happened to him.

RK: [with a sudden and violent snarl] Truck can burn in hell for all I care!

How We Went for Dinner at Reverend Graingers Aunts and What Happened Down at the River Later That Night

Me and Rosie followed along in the Bel Air like before to the next town. Rosie sat real close and we didnt say much and then Rosie asked me if I ever thought about having children again and I have to say it was a real shocker cause I never heard Rosie talk about children before and I never really thought about children after little Becky cause I never thought Id find anyone like Sam ever again. So I told her and she said she understood but she thought about having children sometimes. I know it might sound strange doing what I did and now wanting kids she said. But lots of things have changed for me in the past few months Benny. I said I know and she pressed in real close and I looked out the windshield at the full moon rising and then in the rearview mirror at the sunset. Dont you ever dream of little Bennies running around? she said. Sometimes I guess I said but I didnt really but when she said it I thought it would be okay. Then Rosie touched my neck and kissed my forearm and pretty soon me and Rosie were suckling in the car halfway between the sun and the moon.

Reverend Graingers Aunt Ida lived in the country in a big

house that looked like it might be haunted or something

and I guess she pretty much looked like the ghost that it

might be haunted by cause she was all white but she wasnt

an albino like the reverend but she was just old. Her and

the reverend did have the same small ears and wishbone

kinda nose and the air whistled through Aunt Idas slit

nostrils some when she spoke to me same as the reverends

did. Me and Rosie found a place to sit on a sofa in Aunt Idas

entertaining room and she snapped the heavy curtains

shut in front of the windows and a whole lot of dust came

off them and filled the room. Truck sat across from us and

I could see him looking at a big wooden cross on the wall

above the fireplace that had a layer of dust on it and it

looked pretty much like the one in the Holy Cross Church

except for Jesus was more bloody in this one and I

wondered if Truck was thinking the same thing I was

thinking. I mean Im not real proud of it but the same

night Truck and I broke into the church and Truck did a

dump in the big organ pipe he tried to put his underwear

on the wooden Jesus hanging on the cross on the front

wall of the Holy Cross Church but the underwear wouldnt

go on so he just put it over Jesus head instead. Then he laughed for a long time like maybe he was getting even for something and I wondered what Jesus had ever done to him to deserve that but I guess I was as guilty as Truck cause I held the ladder when he did it and at first I thought it looked pretty funny so I think I laughed some too in the beginning. Anyway I looked real close at Truck to see if he might remember it but I couldnt tell nothing from his face so I thought maybe all Trucks sins really did get washed away when he accepted the Lord into his life cause it seemed like he couldnt even remember them himself no more. Pretty soon Will the piano player walked in the room and sat down by Truck and his head jerked like the way it always did and sometimes made him miss notes while he was playing the piano. Mr. Fairfux says it sounds like a tick but I think Reverend Grainger told me Will the piano player had a stroke once right in the middle of Rock of Ages or something and maybe that was why he jerked like that. The reverend told me Will was one of his first converts too and Will used to play in a Jazz band with a famous saxophone player or something before he changed his sinful ways and found the Lord or the Lord found him I guess. Aunt Idas cook served us a meal of duck and a casserole with mushrooms and maybe asparagus and a few other things I didnt recognize in it and the whole time she was talking about her fiance and how he drowned in the river and her nose was whistling like the way I said it did and the reverends did too. Rosie asked about her fiance and Aunt Ida said he was a preacher just like Reverend Grainger and he liked to take his morning ablutions down at the river and one day he just never came back. The river swept my Douglas away she said and a tear appeared at the corner of her eye. So a little later me and Rosie went down to look at the river and a few other people came along too. The moon was like a big streetlight dripping silver ribbons or something and it lit the trail through the grass. When we got there the river looked like bubbling tar in the moonlight and right about then a few of the others stripped down and were wading into the water and pretty soon Rosie was too. She took my hand and said come on Benny lets swim and I said I dont know. I looked up to the riverbank and Reverend Grainger and Will the piano player were standing there and I wondered what the reverend thought about all of it. I mean I was no expert on sin or nothing but I thought it might be a sin or close to it to be naked in front of other people but then the

reverend said *go on Benny*. The Lord understands he said
but I wasnt sure what the Lord understood exactly but I
went ahead and got undressed anyway and pretty soon I
was locked in Rosies arms. I guess it was right about then
I saw Truck standing in the water up to his waist and
looking at me like he was gonna say something but then he
never did. His body looked real tight and hard compared
with mine and his muscles shone when he turned and
sloshed to shore. Whats wrong? asked Rosie and she rubbed
against me and I could feel my man thing moving around
under the water. Nothing I said. Nothing at all.

September 3

Spent the morning on the Internet trying to track down Reverend James Grainger. Then the afternoon following up on the phone. Found out a couple of interesting things about the reverend, which were helpful in locating him. First, he was a longtime member of AA. And although AA doesn't keep records, an equally longtime member named Beth clearly recalled a tall skinny albino who claimed to be a man of God attending meetings on Folsom Street in the Mission District. But more helpful was the sex offenders registry. Seems the good Reverend couldn't keep his paws off some of the young members of his congregation, one in particular, Nell Faulks, now thirty-four and living in San Diego. The conviction dated back two decades and the Reverend had somehow managed to keep a lid on it. But the sex offenders registry still had him listed at an address near Van Ness Station. The listing was for an office, a rented space in an office complex built in the seventies. From this central location, the Reverend took his revival show up and down the West Coast on at least two extensive tours a year. That is, until the very public incident with Benny became headlines fifteen months ago. So Ray was probably right about Reverend Grainger laying low in San Francisco.

Called the office all afternoon but got no answer. Finally gave up and went for a drink at the Thirsty Bear Saloon.

September 4

Decided to work from my room again today. The throbbing in my head can only be described as something akin to a nuclear fission meltdown. Thought I'd follow up on a lead that came up in yesterday's search for Reverend Grainger. Beth, the same senior AA member who recalled the Reverend, also recalled his old side-kick William the piano player, aka, Willie Boy Boyd, a fixture in the West Coast Cool Jazz scene in the '60s to the early '80s, at which time he joined up with Reverend Grainger's traveling revival show. As luck would have it, Willie still made the occasional appearance at the AA on Folsom, and now had a regular gig at a piano bar named Jerry's. Called Jerry's and got the manager, who was kind enough to give me Willie's home phone number when I told him I was a friend of Willie's agent (to which he responded, "Didn't know the old man had an agent.")

Willie got on the phone, sounding much like me—suffering the indignities of excessive drink. Although I knew he was a faithful AA member, I also knew AA members fell off the wagon on a semi-regular basis. Toads, the other members secretly called them, because of the way they jumped on and off the wagon.

Interview Transcript: Willie Boy Boyd

Me: I'm currently working on a manuscript written by Benjamin Salmon. Much of this memoir concerns his experience with Reverend James Grainger. Do you remember Benny at all?

WB: Ha, 'course I remember Brother Benjamin. How often do you meet a cat like that?

Me: You mean a man that lactates?

WB: Of course, yeah, a cat that lactates. But let spell it out straight to you—it was more than just lactating. When you got Brother Benjamin feeling the spirit, he looked to've sprung a mighty leak or two all over the place, if you know what I mean.

Me: Yes, I think I do. Let's talk for a minute about your relationship with Reverend Grainger. How did you two first meet?

WB: Me and Jay? We first met at The G Spot, a jazz joint on Ocean Avenue, by the pier.

Me: Santa Monica?

WB: That's right. I had a regular gig with a quartet.

Me: Was the Reverend a man of God at the time? Did he have a ministry yet?

WB: Yes and no. He was trying it out, dipping a toe into it at the time. I remember catching sight of him glowing like a pink-eyed ghost in the front booth. His cane looked like the rod of Moses. He had some pretty young thing draped on him. Yes sir, we ended up drinking a bottle of Tennessee whisky that first night. But let me spell it out straight to you—those were drinking days for both of us.

Strictly behind us now. Well maybe not always so strictly, but every day is a new beginning, ain't that right?

Me: So he wasn't a full-fledged man of God at the time, obviously.

WB: Naw. Not like that yet. But it was coming. One night he left The G Spot higher than the King's castle wall. Well, he lost his cane and fell off the pier into the drink. Jay being originally from Texas couldn't swim a lick, you understand, and he thought he was a goner when this angelic-white dolphin picks his sorry self up and pushes him to shore. After that, he quit his sinful ways and turned to the Lord.

Me: Seriously? That's how it happened? A dolphin saved him from drowning? Did you see this yourself?

WB: Course not. I was finishing my last set. He came pounding at the stage door looking like a drowned Chihuahua and prattling on about Jonah and the whale. Let me spell it out straight to you—it was clear enough something happened to him. He looked like he'd seen the face of God.

Me: Wow! That's quite the conversion story. So it wasn't long after that you converted, too?

WB: I'm a Louisiana boy, Mister. Needed no converting, just some reminding, that's all. And Jay—the Reverend—reminded me, brought me back into the fold of our Lord Jesus.

Me: And that's why you joined his revival tours?

WB: As far as I's concerned, the Reverend was heaven sent. A message from above that I should stop my sinful ways and do some good in this world.

Me: Then what do you make of recent events? Of all the accusations against the Reverend and his ministry?

WB: Let me spell it out straight to you, Mister—James Grainger is a man of God. No matter what them papers say. No matter what the critics and the naysayers say. He's done good in this world. And how many people do you know can say that? Can you say that? Can you say you done good in this world?

Me: An interesting question and a good point. Unfortunately, the jury's still out on that one.

The Next Revival Meeting and What Happened There

I stopped at a pay phone the next day and called home to
see how Ray was doing at the new security guard job I got
him. He said Benny I think this is the best job in the whole
darn world and I said I guess and I asked about Rudy. He
said Rudy ODd again last week but he was okay and back at
work. Ive been trying to get him to come around to the Lord
Jesus Christ said Ray and I said good Ray and he said I
dont know Benny but there may not be much hope for Rudy.
I didnt say nothing for a while cause I knew he was pretty
much right but then I finally said I know and I asked about
Phil. Havent seen hide nor hair of Phil said Ray. But I tell
you I could sure use him around here to do some cleaning
up he said. I gotta go Ray I said and he said okay and I hung
up and walked back to the Bel Air. Me and Rosie drove for
another thirty miles or so and everyone pulled over in a
farmers field that was so dry it was like it might go up
in flames if you looked at it too hard or something. I
thought about the time Jarvis Holts field got burned up
when a spark from a train lit it and it burned all day and
night and it looked like it might make it to the Chevy two
ton Truck and his dad lived in. The Chevy was blocked up

so Truck was looking around all day to steal some wheels

in case they needed to push it out of harms way some but

the fire never made it that far. So Truck rolled them

wheels down to Jarvis Holts field and threw them in the

fire just in case someone came looking for them and them

wheels smoked four days straight. Anyway me and Rosie

spent the afternoon putting up posters around the town

and I stopped in at a barber shop to get a shave and a cut

too. The barber said his name was Paulo and he sat me in a

chair and ran a straight razor up and down a leather strop

for a long time and I have to say it made me nervous some

cause he seemed to like sharpening the razor lots more than

I thought he should. He asked me about the poster I put up

on the light standard outside his shop and I said it was

for a revival meeting on the outskirts of town and so he

stepped outside to get a closer look at it. He stood there

for a long time under the barbers pole that just kept

spinning like it was drilling a hole to China or something

and then he came back inside and said whos Benjamin the

Miracle Man? I have to say that I thought about lying to

Paulo and saying it was someone else but then I thought

it would be wrong on a few different counts so I didnt. Im

Benjamin. Benny really I said and I thought about telling

him that the reverend thought people would like
Benjamin better than Benny cause it was a name from the
Bible but I didnt. So what kinda miracles you do Benny?
he asked. Nothing real specific I said. Mostly healing I
guess. Healing? said Paulo. You mean like making the lame
walk and the deaf talk and such as that? he said. The deaf
hear you mean I said. What? said Paulo and he stopped
running the razor up and down and it made me more
nervous than when he was running it up and down real
serious. You said make the deaf talk I said. But I guess
you mean make the deaf hear. No shit! said Paulo. I said
that? Yes I said. Oh he said. Too much hair tonic I guess he
said and he started lathering up his brush on the soap. So
how do you do these miracles then Benny? said Paulo. I have
to say I wasnt real sure how to answer the question but
finally I just said my man-milk. Man-milk? said Paulo.
What do you mean man-milk? So I told Paulo about me and
Rosie and the suckling and how I met Reverend Grainger
and everything that happened after that. When I was
finished it was so quiet I could hear Paulos razor grinding
over the stubble under my chin and I have to say the
silence made me nervous all over again. So what youre
saying is this man-milk of yours makes people better. Is

that about it? said Paulo. Yeah thats about it I said.
Paulo spun me around in the chair so our noses were pretty
much touching and he looked me in the eyes and said my
mommas got a bad ticker. Shes gonna die any day said Paulo.
You think you can heal her heart? I could smell garlic
sausage or some other strong smelling meat on his breath
and it was so strong I couldnt think straight mostly with
him so close. Finally I said I dont know. Maybe. Maybe? he
said. Probably I said. What times the meeting? he asked.
8:30 I answered. Well be there said Paulo.

The crowd this time was bigger than the crowd last time but I
wasnt so nervous this time and me and Rosie sat on the front
row where Reverend Grainger thought we should. Will the
piano player was playing some kinda warm and nice hymn
that sounded like the way a real white goose gliding on a
real clear lake would sound if it was a sound. Something
like that anyway. And every so often Will the piano player
would do one the jerks that he does and he would hit a note
that sounded like something from a whole other song and
it would kinda shock you like when you swallow a hard
seed in your lemon-aid or something. Pretty soon Reverend
Grainger came out through a split in the red felt curtain

and I just saw a flash of Truck when he did and the reverend
walked to the pulpit and set down his white Bible and
clapped his hands in time to the music and little white puffs
of baby powder puffed off his hands when he did. He had his
white hair tied back in a ponytail and his white beard looked
more yellow than usual tonight and I thought maybe it was
the new bulbs we put in the overhead lights when we were
setting things up. He started into his sermon about the
craftiness of the devil when the music stopped and there
was lots of amens in the crowd and I guess I said amen a
time or two even though I was pretty sure the devil didnt
need to be real crafty cause most people just made trouble
for themselves mostly and then ended up sinning to get
out of the trouble they made in the first place. Mr.
Fairfux thinks thats real insightful but I just think
its the way things are. Anyway the sermon went on for a
while and then there was some more singing and by now the
crowd was getting real active I guess and standing on
their feet and clapping lots and some were holding their
hands in the air like they were holding up something
that collapsed on them or was gonna collapse on them or
something. It was right about then I saw Paulo the barber
standing in the back row with his momma at least I

guessed that the old woman standing with two canes and with eyes puffed up with tears was his momma. I felt my stomach kinda shrink like the way cellophane does when you throw it in the fire pit cause I knew Paulo brought her there tonight to see me so I could heal her bad ticker. It made me nervous some but it also made me happy some too cause I knew if I could heal the old womans ticker then I guess maybe I really was something special like reverend Grainger said I was. Anyway the reverend called for the sick and afflicted in the crowd to come forward so Benjamin the Miracle Man could do Gods magic and heal them. I mean I have to say I still wasnt used to the Benjamin the Miracle Man name but right then it sounded pretty good to me and so I stood up real straight and walked to the stage. Mr. Fairfux says a fancy way of saying name is moniker but I think Ill stick with name since Im not much for fancy words. Anyway pretty soon a young fellow in dark glasses stood up and the reverend called him down and when he did Truck walked out into the crowd to help him cause I guess he was blind. The fellow wore real faded jeans and a black leather jacket and I could see the head of a snake tattoo poking out from under the collar of his shirt and it reminded me of a picture I saw in a Jehovahs Witnesses

pamphlet once of a snake kinda slithered around a tree
and a naked man and woman were sleeping under it. Behold
the afflicted said Reverend Grainger and that was my cue
to squirt the fellow with man-milk. I had my jacket off by
now and my nipples stuck through the holes in my white
robe and Rosie stood behind me kinda massaging my man-
boobs and flicking the nipples up and down the way she
liked to do and the way I liked her to do too. Pretty soon
the young fellow took off his dark glasses and I have to
say it was a real shocker cause below his one eye was a
real big mole or tumor or something just hanging there
like a piece of rotten fruit or something. Mr. Fairfux
says it sounds like a gumma and that the young man must
have had syphilis and I dont know for sure but I never
saw anything like it before or since. Anyway pretty soon
man-milk squirted from my nipples all over him and it
got in his mouth and down his chin on onto his leather
jacket and the rest. It was kinda a shocker cause the
young fellow screamed real loud and fell over backwards
and banged his head some and Truck bent down to help him
up but he was real slow getting up and the crowd was real
quiet now and all there was was the piano playing of Will
the piano player. Finally Truck got him to his feet and it

was a real shocker again cause the gumma under his eye
was gone. I mean it was like there was never nothing there
at all and he started feeling around and he couldnt feel
nothing and he kinda screamed again but this time it was
more like the scream of someone who cant believe what
just happened happened. Praise the Lord said the young
fellow in a voice that seemed lots higher than maybe it
should be cause of the way he looked in his leather jacket
and tattoo and all that. Hallelujah said Reverend
Grainger and by now the crowd was clapping and singing
again and I looked at Paulo and he smiled I guess cause
now he had some hope for his momma and her weak ticker
and him and his momma were next in line to be healed by my
man-milk. But right then as they were ready to step
forward Truck slid in front of them and told them that
was all for tonight. I mean I wanted to say something but
I didnt really know what I could say and the words
snagged in my throat like a fish hook or something and
the next thing I knew Reverend Grainger was leading the
crowd in a final hymn but I couldnt stop looking at
Paulos momma and the way the tears spilled out her eyes.
Pretty soon it was all over and Truck pushed me and Rosie
backstage through the split in the curtain and I took one

last look at Paulo and his momma with the weak ticker and I guess I knew right then she wasnt gonna make it much longer. It wasnt like a vision from God or nothing like that. It was more like common sense than anything else I guess. I mean she was old and had a weak ticker and she didnt look real good so it was pretty clear to me when I looked over my shoulder at her that she didnt have lots of time left. Anyway when we got backstage Reverend Grainger was waiting. That was real good Benny he said. I asked him why we stopped before I got to heal Paulo and his momma and I guess I looked pretty angry cause the reverend said Youve got to keep them wanting more. Like it or not Benny this is Gods business but its also show business. And if it takes a little show business to spread the good word then so be it said Reverend Grainger. He put his hand on my shoulder and squeezed a little too hard and I guess I winced some cause I saw a smile spread over Trucks pocked mug. You okay? said the reverend. I guess I said. Good said he and he let go of my shoulder.

September 12

Drove up to Kelso, WA, to find Paulo Battistinni, aka, Paulo the Barber. Wasn't hard to find since there's only one barbershop in town. The shop is old. Didn't have to ask to know it was owned by his father the barber and his grandfather the barber before that. Third generation immigrant was my guess.

Walked in and Paulo waddled toward me, perhaps too eagerly for someone his size. B. didn't exaggerate about his size. His barber smock hung over his prodigious girth like a hacked off bridal gown. Had a moment of controlled panic when I first saw him. Wondered what might happen to me if Paulo didn't like what I'd come to discuss. Explained as tactfully as I could why I was there and asked if he would go on record. He told me to sit down for a shave and I could ask whatever I wanted.

Sounded good until I realized a straight razor would be pressed on or near my throat at any given moment.

Interview Transcript: Paulo Battistinni

Me: You first met Benny right here in your barber shop, correct?

PB: Yeah, that's right. [stretching the strop tightly, then running the straight razor up and down its length with real relish] He came in for a shave.

Me: And what was your impression of him?

PB: My impression? Nothing much. He seemed normal enough–a bit slow on the draw maybe, but normal.

Me: Then what was it about him that convinced you that he could heal your mother?

PB: [taking a long stroke from beneath my chin to my Adam's apple] Nothing. I wasn't convinced. I was desperate. And stranger things have happened, right? So I took momma to the revival meeting thinking we'd roll the dice and see what came up.

Me: But you never got the chance to "roll the dice"as you say.

PB: Nah, but it wouldn't have mattered anyway. The game was rigged from the start. But you probably know all about that.

Me: Actually, I do, yes. [uncertain how to proceed] And how's your mother now? [holding my breath]

PB: Well, let me tell ya, her old ticker's still hanging in there. And it's lucky for the Reverend she's doing all right. 'Cause if she wasn't, he'd be a dead man. Plain and simple.

Me: And Benny? What are your feelings toward Benny now?

PB: I got nothing against Benny. He did what he could, you know? He don't strike me as the kind of guy who trying to pull a fast one. He's an honest guy who got caught in the middle. Anyway, from what I hear things didn't turn out so well for him. We all got our problems to deal with.

What Happened When Ray Came to Visit and Went to a Revival Meeting Too

I guess the revival meeting got under my skin some and I couldnt get Paulos momma out my head and Reverend Graingers saying it was all showbiz didnt seem right to me neither. Maybe I just wanted to shower everyone with my man-milk and heal them. I dont know but I wasnt real good company for the next few days. Rosie tried to make me feel better by saying lots of different things to me about how she wanted to follow Jesus and how she wanted me to follow Jesus with her but none of it seemed to work and every time she tried to suckle I said I didnt feel like it and I could tell Rosie was hurt but I couldnt make myself do it. I guess something happened to me when I looked at Paulos momma with the bad ticker and now all I could think about was her dying on account of me not healing her. Like I said nothing else seemed to matter much to me. It was like my man-boobs ran dry for everything not about Jesus and healing or something. Things were pretty quiet between Rosie and me so I guess it was a good thing Ray showed up when he did. He pulled up to camp in the red Toyota Corolla he bought from Rudy with one hubcap and one

headlight and wipers worn down to the metal. I have to
say that part of me was worried Ray maybe turned back
into the old Ray since the last time I saw him. Like maybe
whatever it was Reverend Grainger did to him wore off
mostly and he was my pot-smoking ass-pancaking
stepbrother again. But when he got out of the car and
walked over to our camp table looking real normal I
guess I could tell right away he was still the Ray who
found Jesus in the pokey while some cons were reaming out
his rear end and I have to say that it was a real relief. I
asked him what he was doing way out here and he said Way
out here? Youre less than a hundred miles from the city
Benny. I guess it was a real shocker and I looked a bit
surprised cause Ray laughed and said I never had a head
for directions. Youve just been circling the city like a
holy rolling asteroid said Ray. Yeah I guess I said and
laughed cause I thought a holy rolling asteroid sounded
pretty funny. Hows the prosilatizing game? said Ray. The
what? I said. You know he said. Converts and healing the
sick. That kinda thing. Oh I said. Pretty good I guess.
Right then I wanted to tell Ray about Paulo and his momma
with the weak ticker and how Truck stopped me from
healing her but Truck was hanging around and I didnt

wanna say nothing about it in front of him. Truck said hello with a nod of his head and Ray did the same too. I was thinking that maybe Truck would leave then but he sat there cleaning his nails with his jackknife mostly. Rudy okay? I asked. Yeah said Ray. Okay but nothing more. You know he said and I guess I did. The job? I asked. The same said Ray. You know. Right about then Rosie came over and wrapped Ray in her arms and gave him a kiss on the cheek. Well thats the nicest welcome Ive had in some time said Ray. I slipped my arm around Rosie. You two look real good together he said. I guess I went red some cause the truth was things werent so good between us right then. Ray laughed and Rosie said we sure do dont we? And right then I thought of mom and dad but Im not real sure why exactly. I wasnt too young before dad left to live like a black bear in the Rockies to notice how they looked together. I remember seeing dad sweep mom into his arms and her squealing and giggling some and the truth is its like a picture in my head or something now cause I see his bright white undershirt and shiny black hair and her swaying in her flowered dress and the loose blond curls of her hair floating like golden seaweed or something. But mom and Jack didnt really look nothing like that together. I guess they looked like two people trying to scramble out of the same ice hole on the river at the same time and one comes real near to getting out and the other pulls them back in and it just keeps going back and forth like that until finally someone goes under for good. Anyway I guess I never thought of how me and Rosie looked together before Ray said it. Just then Truck stepped forward and said Reverend Grainger wanted to see me and Ray so we left and I looked over my shoulder and saw Rosie and Truck talking and I have to say it bothered me some. When me and Ray got on the reverends bus the two of them shook hands real warm and it looked like they might hug or something but they didnt. Sit down said the reverend. Sit down. Please. Me and Ray found a seat beneath a big fish that wasnt a real fish but was a chrome outline of a fish or something. I didnt know it then but Mr. Fairfux says its an ancient Greek symbol that was used by early Christians and today it is an icon for American Protestant Christianity. Its really great to see you Ray said the reverend. Ive been thinking about you lately. Ray seemed to like that the reverend was thinking about him and he said Ive been thinking about you too Reverend and it seemed like maybe a gay thing to say to me but I guess Ray

didnt know what else to say and thats something I feel
lots of times too. How is life on the outside? asked the
reverend. Still following our Lord and Savior? Oh yeah
definitely said Ray and he half smiled like he wasnt
sure if the reverend was serious or not. You know Im not
one to beat around the bush said the reverend so Ill just
come out and say what I wanna say. Okay said Ray. I want
you to stay and help us spread the good word Ray said the
reverend. We could use a good man like you around here.
Truck could use some help with security at the meetings.
Ray looked surprised and pretty soon he looked like he
might cry or something. He turned his head to me and said
What do you think Benny? and I said sounds good to me.
What about the security guard job? he asked. Quit I said.
Its nothing special. I dont care if I never see another
close-circuit monitor in my life I said. Yeah said Ray
and then he slapped me on the shoulder like I never
remember him doing before and for the first time ever I
felt like we were real brothers mostly even though Phil
always said we werent. So what do you say Ray said
Reverend Grainger. I say all right said Ray. Praise the
Lord said the reverend. Yes praise the Lord said Ray.

Ray made some phone calls and I guess the guys in security werent real happy about the way Ray just kinda dropped his job. No worries said Ray. When Jesus said to Peter and James and John follow me they dropped their nets and followed said Ray. They didnt worry about who was gonna take their shifts until they got a replacement. I guess I knew Ray was probably right about that but it still didnt seem real right to me and part of me thought it was kinda like something the old Ray would do. I mean I thought Ray should quit if he wanted to but I guess I didnt think he should quit right then from a phone booth. Rosie wasnt saying much about nothing but I knew she liked Ray and I guess she wasnt gonna mind having him around. Pretty soon Truck came up to our camp and pulled up a log and said to Ray I hear youre joining us. Ray grinned and said thats right. Praise the Lord. Yeah praise him said Truck and he grinned real wide like the way someone grins before they take a swing at you or something. Rosie slid over some and huddled close to me like the way you do when youre waiting for a bottle rocket to take off or something and I remembered seeing her and Truck talking and I wondered if Truck said something to her she didnt like. I never got time to ask

cause a couple minutes later we all went to bed and Rosie
was asleep as soon as her head hit the pillow. Later that
night I woke up cause I thought I heard footsteps around
our tent so I listened real hard but then they stopped.
The next day I wasnt really sure what I heard so I asked
Ray if he was walking around last night and he said he
never got out of the old Corolla. I guess I was bothered by
it some but then I forgot about the whole thing when it
was time to get ready for the revival meeting. Me and Ray
pitched in to get the big tent up and Rosie found an iron
and ironed Rays pants with a sharp crease that could
slice oranges and flattened the tie he borrowed from
Reverend Grainger. Before long the tent was full and the
meeting started and the crowd was real excited like all
the other nights and Ray said they were all full of the
spirit. I thought about it for a bit and I wasnt sure what
came first being excited or being full of the spirit so I
asked Ray but he said it didnt matter cause it all ended
the same. Hows that? I asked. With these good people coming
to Christ the Lord said Ray. Amen said Rosie and she kinda
pulled on my arm like she was trying to remind me she was
there or something and I turned to her and smiled.
Reverend Grainger came out and talked about repentance

and about washing away sin and the crowd seemed to like

it well enough cause they shouted lots of hallelujahs

and praise the Lords. I guess it was pretty much like the

other meetings except this time when it came time for me

to do my healing Truck and Ray rushed me up to the front

so my feet barely touched the ground and somewhere in

all the excitement I let go of Rosies hand and pretty soon

I was moving away from her and she was left behind like

when youre being pulled down the rapids of a river hanging

on to a log and you can just barely see the person on the

edge that tried to rescue you with a branch. I guess what

Im trying to say is its a pretty sick feeling that ties

your stomach all up like the way you keep tying a shoelace

that just keeps breaking or something. Anyway I tried to

get free from Truck and Ray but I couldnt and then I

looked over my shoulder and I saw Rosie standing there

and I could tell she wondered if she should come up on her

own or not but I guess she thought no cause she didnt come

up and she just watched like everyone else. The truth was

I knew I could make man-milk without her cause I did it

before. All I had to do was think about her real hard and

that made it all happen real easy but it felt strange

being up there on the stage without Rosie flicking my

nipples though the holes in my robe. But I didnt have
much time to think about it cause the sick and afflicted
came at me full bore pretty soon after that and I didnt
even wait for Reverend Grainger to say something about
Benjamin the Miracle Man but I just shot them all with my
man-milk like the way you hose down your friends on a
blistering hot day. Pretty soon they all got better. I
mean I have to say it was a pretty amazing night mostly
even though Rosie wasnt there with me and I healed lots
of people and they all cried and praised the Lord and
blessed me and I guess I was happy and filled with the
spirit too. I guess it was around the end of the meeting
that I looked down to where Rosie was standing earlier
but she wasnt there no more. She was gone and there was
nothing there but a big kinda blank space in the crowd
and I guess Id be lying if I said it didnt make me feel
real sad all of a sudden. And I couldnt stop thinking
that Rosied disappeared but I hoped it wasnt forever.

September 17

Finally got someone to answer the phone at Reverend Grainger's office near Van Ness Station. Young sounding man, named Tobin. Pleasant, almost effeminate. Not a convict. Was sure of that. Asked to speak to the Reverend. Got a stock response—not available but if I leave a number he'll call back. Decided to try and get some answers out of Tobin.

Interview Transcript: Tobin Marx

Me: Can you tell me when the Reverend will be touring the West Coast again?

TM: Reverend Grainger is no longer actively touring.

Me: So he's inactively touring.

TM: No, sir. He not touring at all at this time.

Me: But he's still involved with his ministry?

TM: Not actively, sir.

Me: So inactively, then.

TM: No, not at the moment.

[The line goes silent and I hear a muffled conversation, a seemingly animated one.]

TM: Reverend Grainger has just arrived and will now take your call.

Me: Thank you, Tobin.

[A new voice crackles in my ear—gentler than I would have expected, yet with a nasally sibilance adding a sharpened edge to certain stressed words.]

RJG: This is Reverend James Grainger. Who am I speaking to?

Me: My name is Derek Gettelman. I'm working with Benny Salmon on a book that he has written. Some of the events in that book concern you. In the interest of presenting a fair and balanced account of those events, I'd like to ask you a few questions.

RJG: I'm afraid I can't answer any of your questions concerning any events, as legal proceedings are in the works and my lawyer has advised me to talk to no one.

Me: I see. Perhaps, then, we can find some neutral ground. Benny–uh, Brother Benjamin–says nothing about your past in his book, presumably because he knew nothing of your past. Would you at least indulge me in a few facts about you? Where you came from? Why you got into the ministry? Things like that.

RJG: Look, what do you want me to say? That my pappy was a scoundrel landlord in Tallapoosa County, getting rich off the back-breaking labor of sharecroppers? And my mamma drank mint juleps all day and was abusive to the help in out Southern manor? I could say that but it wouldn't be true. And being a man of God, the truth is still important to me. Truth is the only kind of commerce that really matters between two people. So here's the truth. I was born and raised in Hoboken, New Jersey, the only child to middle-class parents who made ends meet well enough. My father never rose above assistant manager at the small bank where he worked his whole life and my mother was a homemaker all of her life. I wasn't beaten or abused at home. I was treated kindly at the best of times and indifferently at the worst. Being albino, I was homeschooled so as not be bullied or made-to-feel small by the cruelties of other children.

Me: So what prompted you to take up the Good Book and become a man of God, as you say?

RJG: In a word: girls. I didn't have the looks or the talent to be an Elvis, so I took an alternate route to notoriety, if not fame. In time, however, the girls became less important and the Good Word took hold of me. I self-converted on the job, I guess you could say. [The line goes silent again. More muffled conversation] I'm afraid that's all the questions I have time for. Any further queries should be directed to my legal counsel.

Me: Let me just ask you one final thing, one very important thing. Did Benny's man-milk really heal you? Or was that all just part of your plan?

RJG: [slight pause, sighing deeply, perhaps with resignation] Son, all I can tell you is I spent the greater portion of my life in a haze of half-blindness. And now I can see—for the first time things around me are clear. Call it an awakening of sorts. Call it a miracle if you wish. Was it Benny's man-milk? The truth is—I don't know. Was it God? Yes. Of that I feel certain.

How I Found Out Rosie Was Gone and What Happened after That

Mr. Fairfux says this part of the story is the lead-up to the climax and the climax is a point of high dramatic tension and major turning point in the story when everything comes to a head and I guess thats right cause things pretty much come to a head real soon just like Mr. Fairfux says. I left the big tent after the meeting and looked for Rosie but I couldnt find here nowhere. I looked in our tent and I couldnt see any of her things and her bag was gone too so I looked in the car and there was nothing there neither. I guess I was moping some cause Will the piano player asked me what the matter was and I told him Rosie disappeared and I didnt know where she went. Will said she was likely gone home and I asked him why he thought so and he said he saw her out on the road trying to hitch a ride west. I thought about it some and then I wondered how Will saw her and I didnt so I asked and he said he was out for a cigarette between my healing the blind girl and healing the man with jake leg and I said oh I see. Ya better get looking for her hadnt ya said Will and I said yeah I guess I had and I got in the Bel Air and headed west on the highway and the headlights were

long and kinda sad in front of me and I remembered how

mom used to come home from the Thirsty Bear and pack me

in the car some nights after dad left to live like a black

bear in the Rockies and we drove up and down the back

roads looking for him. I guess in her drunk state mom got

it in her head that dad was wandering the countryside

trying to find his way home or something. I didnt know

for sure what she was hoping for but I remember the way

she had both hands on the wheel at ten and two just where

dad always said they should be and she drove down the

middle of the road and gravel was crunching under the

tires and flipping up into the wheel wells and she was

pretty much looking up and down both ditches like her

life depended on it or something. When we finally got

back to the house Jack was always sleeping in front of

the TV with his pill bottles same as he always was so he

never knew nothing about it and never said nothing about

it to mom or me neither. Anyway I drove fifteen miles or so

I guess looking for Rosie but she was gone so I thought

someone mustve picked her up and gave her a ride home. I

thought shed have to go back to the house cause she didnt

have an apartment no more so I stopped at a phone booth

and called but no one answered. I guess I called about ten
times that night and didnt get no one at home so I thought
she wasnt there yet or maybe she wasnt ever gonna be there
again. And I have to say that the thought of her never being
there again made me real sad and my man-boobs starting
leaking all over like they were crying for her or something
so I sat down and my belly sloughed over my pants and I sat
there and I wondered what to do next.

———

I tried to call some more the next morning but got no answer
again so I went to talk to Reverend Grainger about what to
do. He felt sad too mostly but I guess not as sad as me and he
said the Lord sometimes expects us to make sacrifices so
the work can go forward. Ray was there too and he said a
quiet amen and I guess that meant he agreed with the
reverend. The show must go on I said and I guess I sounded
bitter some cause Reverend Grainger said dont think of it
that way Benny. Think of it as storing up treasures in
heaven. What treasures? I asked and I was trying not to
sound bitter no more. The treasures that the Lord will
surely lay at your feet for sacrificing for Him right
here and now upon this earth. Oh I said but the truth was
I didnt really care about treasures right then. Take the

afternoon to think about it said the reverend. But be
ready to heal some poor souls tonight. Its your calling
Benny. Its why the Lord put you here on the earth he said
and he looked like he meant it and I maybe believed him
once but I wasnt sure if it was true no more. Anyway I did
what the reverend said and I spent the afternoon thinking
about it. I found a grove of cherry trees nearby and sat
down and thought about what the Lord wanted me to do and
what I wanted to do cause the truth was part of me wanted
to go back to Rosie but part of me wanted to stay on the
road and heal poor souls with my man-milk. I guess I
couldnt stop thinking about them sick people and who
would heal them if I didnt.

That night was a meeting like none other before. I healed
close to twenty people I guess and every one of them sang
praises to the Lord and thanked me and my man-milk and
the reverend for doing the Lords work here on earth. I
guess it was the first time in my life that I ever felt
really useful and like maybe people liked me some too. I
mean like I said before I was popular for a couple months
one summer when I was a kid and I got my purple banana-
seat bike but I knew that the other kids didnt really like

me so much as they liked my bike. But these meeting and the healings were different than that cause I knew I was really doing something to help them sick and afflicted people. The night after that was the same and the night after that too and the meetings were getting real full and people were coming from all around to be healed by Benjamin the Miracle Man and people that saw me on the streets of their town knew it was me. And I guess pretty soon I never thought much about Rosie no more. I mean I thought about her at first to get the man-milk flowing but pretty soon I didnt even have to do that no more cause I just thought about healing people and the man-milk pretty much just came. I guess the truth was I thought about Rosie some nights when I was laying in the tent alone and I wondered how she was and what she was doing but before long I would fall asleep and she would disappear into the blackness again.

September 20

Half asleep on my bed when I got a phone call from Gavin. Wasn't prepared so had nothing ready to say. Listened mainly. Don't know why exactly, but I clicked the red button on my mini tape recorder and held it to the phone. Wanted everything on record? Maybe.

Interview Transcript: Gavin Whitehead

GW: I know you've been trying to get a hold of me, and this is the hardest phone call I've ever had to make, Derek. You've got to know that, OK?

Me: [saying nothing]

GW: I hoped that once the play closed and I said I was going back to Missouri that you'd just give up and quit calling. But you didn't.

Me: [saying nothing]

GW: Can't you say something?

Me: So who is he?

GW: Does it matter?

Me: Yes and no. Mostly yes.

GW: It's John.

Me: Fairfax?

GW: Yes. Are you surprised?

Me: Yes and no. Mostly no.

GW: I'm sorry, Derek. I didn't want to hurt you. But you know things with us weren't really going anywhere.

Me: Actually, I didn't know that. Now I do.

GW: John is very worried that this will make your working relationship weird. That's why I didn't tell you earlier. [short but pregnant pause] So, how is the book coming?

Me: It's fine. And you can tell John not to worry. I'm just about ready to wrap up the research. I'm flying back to New York on Monday to start writing.

GW: He'll be relieved to hear that.

Me: Just tell me one thing. Did I get this job because of you? Was it only to get me out of the city long enough for you two to get together?

GW: Of course not. You got the job because you were qualified to do it. You've been working the last ten years for an opportunity like this. And you finally got it. That's the truth.

Me: Someone once told me that truth is the only kind of commerce that really matters between two people. At the time, I didn't fully understand what he meant. Now I do.

GW: Derek . . .

Clicked off the tape recorder and hung up. Dropped down onto the bed and closed my eyes. Felt like I could sleep. Really sleep. For the first time since arriving, for the first time in a long time, I let my mind go blank and I drifted off, slowly at first, into a calm Morphean dreamscape.

How I Tried to Heal Paulo the Barbers Momma and Everything Came to a Head

It was right about this time I first noticed Truck disappeared too. I mean it seemed strange to me that he disappeared about the same time Rosie did but I never really put the two things together like they were connected or something. I remembered Truck was always coming and going anyways so it pretty much didnt mean nothing to me right then. At least thats what I told myself. He mustve had enough of the Lord said Ray. I guess so I said. I always wondered if he was just using it as a way to get out of the pokey early said Ray. Me too I said and I felt guilty some cause I guess I used to think maybe Ray was doing the same thing. Anyway we both thought it was probably better that Truck was gone cause he made everyone feel uneasy mostly. I guess it was the night after I noticed Truck was gone that I made another discovery and it changed pretty much everything for me.

The meeting that night was like all the others and Reverend Grainger gave a sermon that sounded like all the others too cause it was about sin and repentance and finding the Lord. I guess I understood a while back that the message is pretty much the same and it never really changes mostly from one town to the next and I guess that makes sense cause Christ the Lord never changes neither except in the pictures on the cover of the Jehovahs Witnesses pamphlets. Anyway after the reverend got the crowd going real good it was time for me to get on stage and start healing the poor afflicted souls with my man-milk. I guess I was happy to see Paulo in the crowd again and I watched him get up and help his momma with the weak ticker up and she walked real unsteady up to the stage but before she made it a young fellow stepped in front of her and limped his way up the aisle. I was real mad at this happening again and I looked to Reverend Grainger cause I was thinking he might do something about it but he welcomed the young fellow up on to the stage the same as last time. I looked down into Paulos face and I could see he was ready to explode or worse but I guess he didnt cause we were in a house of God or at least a tent of God. Anyway the young fellow had a withered limb and I thought it must have been from polio or something and he dragged his leg across the stage and I remember thinking he moved pretty good for someone with a withered limb. I

pulled my robe tight and thought about the Lord and His
goodness and pretty soon the man-milk was spraying
everywhere and by everywhere I mean all over the young
fellow with the withered limb. Be healed said Reverend
Grainger real loud and it sounded deep and wavy like one
of them fat men who sings opera or something and the
young fellow kicked his leg up and starting dancing real
fast right there and it was right about then I saw the
snake tattoo poking from under his collar. I have to say
it took a minute to sink in but pretty soon I remembered
seeing it before cause was the same tattoo that made me
think of the Jehovahs Witnesses pamphlet with the snake
slithered around the tree and the naked man and woman
below it. Then I remembered the young fellow with the
withered leg was the same blind young fellow in a leather
jacket and ripped jeans that I healed two weeks or so before
I guessed. And I stood there and the milk was squirting
from both my man-boobs and it was kinda slowing down
like the way it slows down near the end of your making pee
water or something. I looked over at Ray and he was
clapping and singing and yelling Hallelujah and I
looked over at the reverend and his white hair looked
like a waterfall of light and his beard was like a shiny

pool beneath it or something. I guess an anger started in the heels of my shoes and it just climbed up my legs and past my stomach and up to my gullet and finally came to a boil in my brain cause I grabbed the young fellow who was supposed to have a withered leg but didnt have a withered leg and who was blind last time I saw him and I threw him off the stage. I mean Im no strong man like the way the guy at the carnival presses a drunk Irishman over his head or something but Im not a weak man neither I guess cause I mustve tossed the faker a good three rows into the audience. I guess Paulo figured something wasnt right neither cause he pushed by his momma with the weak ticker and he belted the faker with his big iron barbers fists and blood started squirting from the young fellows nose and mouth. Pretty soon Ray was on Paulos back trying to get him off but Paulo shrugged his big wide shoulders and sent Ray flying like he was a tiny fly or something. It seemed like a long time before Paulo finally stopped and by then the crowd cleared out of the tent mostly except for a few of us. Me and Ray and the Reverend and Will the piano player. And Paulos momma with a weak ticker was there too and she sat and watched like it was something that happened all the time or something. Anyway Paulo

led his momma out without saying a word and it left the
rest of us looking at each other and looking at the bloody
young fellow on the floor. Reverend Grainger got down
off the stage and started to tend to hurt faker with a
kinda tenderness I never saw from him before. I guess it
was right about then I noticed the resemblance. The
reverend and the young man had the same small ears and
wishbone nose and the air whistled though the bloody
slits of his nose like the way the reverends did and like
Aunt Idas did too. Who is that I asked but I guess I already
knew the answer. Hes my son said the reverend and he took a
hanky from his pocket and pressed it to the young mans
nose and he groaned real loud. Why is he pretending to be
lame when last time he was pretending to be blind? I
asked. Reverend Grainger sighed real loud and said we
didnt want you to notice Benny. We thought it was better
not to tell you. We? I said and I looked over at Ray and a
memory of him pushing his ass-pancake against the front
window of our house popped into my head. We said the
reverend. Truck and I. Ray didnt know nothing about it so
dont blame him. I guess what he said was the truth cause
Ray looked more surprised than me about the whole thing.
All part of the show I guess I said and Reverend Grainger

got to his feet and looked kinda sad and angry both and said it wasnt just a show Benny. Its the Lords work too but sometimes the Lord needs a little help getting people to believe in him. So you faked the healings I said. No Benny no! he said. Not all of them. Some of them like Jacobs they were arranged. And that was only to get things started. Once people saw what your man-milk could do for them then they believed and were healed. But what they saw wasnt real I said. So they believed in something made up or something not true. Something arranged. The reverend spread his arms wide like the way he did in his sermons and said But does it matter if it brought them to the Lord and it healed their afflictions? Your man-milk is a gift from God Benny. Your man-milk healed those people said the reverend. No them people healed themselves I said. They wanted to believe it so bad they healed themselves and it wouldnt matter who sprayed them with milk or anything else even I said and I turned around real fast and walked down the aisle of the tent. Dont be that way Benny said Reverend Grainger. God has a calling for you. I turned and said Im not interested no more. Im sorry Reverend Grainger but Im just not interested.

———

Ray walked with me to the Bel Air and asked me where I was going and what I was gonna do next. I told him I had to find Rosie and I knew I was wrong to let her go. I know said Ray. Good luck. I loaded the tent into the trunk and asked Ray what he was gonna do. Im gonna stay Benny. You know the reverend changed my life and hes not a bad man. Hes doing a good thing Benny. I know I said. You should stay. Come home whenever you like. I started up the Bel Air and put it into gear and drove off. I guess I didnt know if Ray would ever come back to the house and park his Corolla on my new driveway and stay at the house again but I hoped he would. I mean I really hoped he would. He was my brother after all.

September 29

Checked out of the Pinewood Lodge this morning. Caught a bus out of Seattle to Coeur D'Alene. My last stop on the way back to NYC. Finally tracked down Rosie/Norma's mother there. My first time in Idaho. Wondered if it was as wild west as they say it is.

Took a taxi to a small war-time house with bare wooden siding and an overgrown lawn. A gray, slim and slightly bent lady answered the door. I told her we'd spoken on the phone and she invited me in. Tea was ready, waiting on the coffee table. The front room was crowded with too much furniture and the walls were covered with crafts and knickknacks that one buys at a country bazaar. There were photos too. Of just one girl–from toddler to teen, photos in ascending chronological order. Until they stopped abruptly, it seemed, somewhere around sixteen.

Interview Transcript: Rosalie McCully

Me: Thank you for speaking to me today, Mrs. McCully. As I said on the phone, I'm working on a book and your daughter Norma is an important part of that book.

RM: I was so surprised to get your call. I haven't heard my daughter's name spoken out loud in so many years. [starting to tear up] Agent Carmichael told us to be prepared for the worst. He said she was probably dead. But I never gave up hope.

Me: When was the last time you saw Norma?

RM: Seventeen years ago. She was fifteen when we sent her to her Aunt Laura's in Seattle.

Me: Do you mind me asking why you sent her there . . . to Seattle?

RM: Well, it's complicated, I suppose. Artie and I were mixed up with the Sun Cloud Clan at the time. [looking straight into my eyes, speaking sternly almost defiantly] Have you heard of the Sun Cloud Clan?

Me: Just that it's something of a death cult.

RM: Yes, well, that's right. Back then, it all made sense to Artie and me. We knew that one day Master Borealis would ask us to make the ultimate sacrifice. And we were willing, but we didn't want our baby involved.

Me: So you sent her away.

RM: Yes. Artie and me went to Montreal to be with Master Borealis and the Clan on the final journey.

Me: Obviously, you didn't make that final journey.

RM: No–no, I didn't. My faith faltered at the last minute. When I saw my Artie lying lifeless on the floor, not looking like he was being transmigrated anywhere, I changed my mind. Something in me snapped to, woke up, and I knew it was wrong . . . all wrong.

Me: You were able to get away from Master Borealis?

RM: He died with the rest of them. Rumor has it his death was accidental, though. He got his glass mixed up with someone else's and he ended up drinking arsenic instead of cool berry Kool Aid.

Me: What happened after that?

RM: I came back to Idaho and started looking for Norma. I looked for thirteen years. And even though Agent Carmichael said I shouldn't get my hopes up, I never stopped looking. Then I got your phone call.

Me: Do you plan to fly out to Seattle to see her . . . Norma?

RM: I don't know how she'd feel about it, but I'm thinking that way. When you've wanted something so badly for so long and you suddenly–unexpectedly–get it, sometimes you don't know what to do with it. I suppose that's how I'm feeling right now. And if I learned one thing from the Sun Cloud Clan experience, it's know what you're getting yourself into before you get yourself into it.

Me: How much do you know about what Norma's life has been like for the past seventeen years?

RM: Only what you've told me. I suppose it's been hard for her. These last thirteen years, there've been countless night's lying awake, wondering if she was out there, and thinking about the things she must've had to do to survive. I'm sure she wasn't proud of those things. I only hope she had moments of happiness along the way, even if only fleeting moments.

Me: I can assure you Mrs. McCully that Norma has known at least some small degree of happiness. She has loved and has been loved.

RM: [tears trailing over her gaunt cheeks] Thank you. I'm a silly old woman–yes, it's true. But I still believe there is no greater happiness than love. I hope my baby knows it too.

How I Found Rudy First and then Rosie and Truck and What Happened After That

I drove straight to Orions Belt My Ass and went inside to look for Rosie but I didnt see her nowhere so I sat down and I ordered a beer. I guess part of me was glad I didnt find her cause I thought if I did find her she might be with another guy and it would pretty much break my heart clean in two if I did. But I did find Rudy inside. I mean I didnt really expect to find Rudy but when I thought about it it was real natural for him to be there cause it was two in the morning and he was still working across the street and I guess he was still coming over here for drinks about every night. I could tell right away that he was huffing his special blend of cleaning solutions that night cause his eyes were more beady than usual or at least more beady than I remembered them being before. Benny! My man! said Rudy and he slid from his chair and fell onto the floor so I helped him back in his seat and I said Hey Rudy. Last I heard you was savin souls with your man-boobs or some fuckin crazy thing like that said Rudy. Yeah something like that I said. Look Rudy I said. I cant really talk right now. Im looking for someone. Rudy leaned in close and I could smell ammonia or something on him and he said You lookin for that tasty piece a black ass am I right he said. I guess I coulda knocked him down easy enough but I didnt wanna at least not right now. Instead I just said yeah Rudy you seen her? Yeah I seen her in here a while back with some white dude he said. A fuckin con for sure. He had the look said Rudy. I guess I finally put the two things together in my head after all this time. Rosie disappearing and Truck taking off right after. My stomach tightened up till it was so tight I had to bend over my beer and I mean Ive never been gut shot before but I guessed being gut shot woulda felt something like it. Where did they go? I asked. No idea said Rudy but I guess I already knew where they went. Thanks Rudy I said. Lets have a drink one day. Rudy straightened up as good as he could and said sure thing Benny. Sure thing.

I got a tire iron from the trunk of the Bel Air and I walked to the Kings Head Hotel. I marched past the old guy at the front desk that looked like he shaved with a sardine can lid or something and went up the stairs to room 212. I have to say I didnt know what I was gonna do mostly cause I wasnt thinking real straight at all. I guess I just needed to

see Rosie and I needed to get her away from Truck cause I
knew Truck and I knew what he was like. I mean I knew him
lots of years ago and I guess I thought he was worse now
than before and I thought him going to jail sort of
proved that point real good. Anyway I pried the door open
and walked in but as soon as I did I felt something hard
crack across my back and I fell to the ground like a sawn
tree and I felt like my lungs popped or something cause I
couldnt catch my breath at all. I groaned real loud and
after a while I rolled over and I saw Truck standing
there grinning and he had a broken broom handle in his
hands and then I heard a scream and I knew right away it
was Rosie. So I looked over to the bed and I saw her there
naked in the sheets and I felt a dribble from my nipple
and then another and another and the man-milk ran down
the inside of my jacket and soaked the shirt Rosie cut up
for me before. I guess right then I pretty much didnt care
if I died or not cause the feeling that thumped in my
chest was like none I ever felt before and it was worse
than the feeling I had when I thought Rosie disappeared
from my life forever. Right about then a foot hit my ribs
and I heard a crack and a sharp pain made me groan again
louder this time. Benny Benny said Truck and it was a

kinda growl more than anything. Who invited you he said
but I was still looking at Rosie and I wanted to say
something like Im sorry but I couldnt get the words out.
Did you come here to heal me too said Truck and then he
laughed loud like the way someone laughs when they want
people to notice them but not laugh too. Or did you come
here to heal your whore said Truck. Speak up he yelled and
he kicked me again and I heard another crack and I groaned
again real loud. No Benny you had your chance to heal the
whore and you failed. You fucked it up like you fuck
everything up. Yeah I know about your marriage said Truck.
You fucked that up too. Come to think of it Benny youve
been a fuck up as long as I can remember. I looked at Rosie
and the milk was running down my shirt and the tears
were running down my face. Rosie I said. You told him.
Benny Im sorry she said. It was nothing. He is nothing.
Truck took a couple of giant steps across the room and
grabbed Rosie by the hair. She told me everything Benny.
Everything he said and he shook her head and Rosie
whimpered and he threw her off the bed and there was a
kinda wet splat as her head hit the floor. I tried to crawl
for the tire iron but Truck jumped on me and put his hard
dry hands around my throat and he started to squeeze real

tight. Pretty soon I could see black bubbles popping before my eyes and I thought it was the end right there in the Kings Head Hotel. But then I thought about Rosie and I wondered if she was all right and I wanted to go to her and to hold her and to make her better. Maybe I missed my chance to heal her like Truck said but I wanted one more chance real bad and as I thought it my man-boobs started to shoot kinda soft at first but gaining strength until they were shooting real hard and the man-milk shot right in Trucks eyes and he kinda screamed and acted like the way the wicked witch did when Dorothy threw water on her. Anyway pretty soon his grip loosened on my throat and without thinking I reached out and grabbed the tire iron and hit Truck square in the temple with it and it made a terrible sound like a kinda sickening thud. I guess I knew I killed him right then and there cause he pretty much folded in half and he fell over onto my chest and my man-milk kept pouring over him and wouldnt stop. I finally pushed Truck off and crawled to Rosie and pulled her close and the blood from her head covered my hands and the floor and the man-milk from my man-boobs showered her with yellowy white milk and it mixed with her blood and made a kinda pink paste on the floor. So I pulled her close and

tried to get her to suckle and her eyes kinda fluttered
and rolled in her head but I kept trying to get her to take
my nipple between her teeth like the way she used to do
but she couldnt not matter how hard I tried. And I guess
it was about then that I heard footsteps coming loud up
the stairs and I heard voices and I knew it was the police
just like I knew that my life was never gonna be the same
again no matter if Rosie lived or died but I wanted her to
live more than anything else in the world right then. So
I held her real tight and I waited to see what came next.

September 30

Landed at JFK early afternoon. All my notes, recording, B.'s manuscript in my brief case. Didn't bother to wait for my luggage. Didn't care. Maybe I'd pick it up later. Took a taxi home. Home to an empty apartment. The tomb-like silence of home. Nothing there but the blinking light of the answering machine. No trace of Gavin. His clothes were gone. Bathroom was cleaned out. Even his favorite Betty Boop coffee mug had vanished from the kitchen cupboard.

Went to work immediately on B.'s manuscript. Writing kept my mind off things. Things. Off Gavin. Part of me hoped he call. Come back. Part of me didn't. Strange to feel so torn about how I want things to happen. Therein lay the source of my weakness. Torn in two.

Sitting in front of the computer searching for a word on the tip of my tongue. Recalled how Gavin would call them out until eventually he'd hit on the one I was looking for.

Fissile. Yes, fissile. Capable of or prone to being split or divided in the direction of the grain or along natural planes of cleavage. My fissile nature. Our fissile relationship.

Halfway through the first chapter by nine p.m. Stopped for a drink. Nothing but Kahlua in the cupboard. Sloshed some into a glass and added skim milk of questionable integrity and possible morbidity. Thought about J.F. Wondered if he'd it planned it all along. My exit. Considered quitting the project. Not writing the book. Throwing out all my notes, transcripts. Quashing all my ideas about how to tell B.'s story and leaving NYC. But I knew I couldn't. B.'s is a story I want to tell. A remarkable story that had nothing to do with J.F. With Gavin. Or with me.

Reached for my tape recorder and turned it on. I began to talk.

Interview Transcript: Derek Gettelman

Me: I understand you're working on an important project. One that could change the trajectory of your career in the publishing industry.

DG: That's right, yes. It happened quite suddenly. Rather unexpectedly. At least, for me it was unexpected.

Me: And what have you learned from this project?

DG: How long have you got? [laughing]

Me: As long as you want to take. [laughing] Seriously, what did you learn?

DG: I don't quite know yet. It takes time to process and compartmentalize. But I can tell you I did learn something.

Me: Ah yes, the writerly instinct, is it not? Internalize? Compartmentalize?

DG: Perhaps.

Me: What's next, then, for Derek Gettelman?

DG: What's next? Well, finish this book. See it through to publication. Then take a few months off. After that, I don't know. Maybe I'll take a few classes. Learn to cook. Learn to dance. Self-improvement, you know? And eventually, eventually, maybe I'll try writing something of my own. Some fiction, perhaps. I think I'd like that. What is it they say about books and writing? Ah yes, "Everyone has a book in them." We'll see about that, won't we?

What Happened After That and Pretty Much
Right Up Until Now

So I guess that was the climax like Mr. Fairfux said and
now is the conclusion. Mr. Fairfux says the ending of the
story is where conflicts are resolved but I guess for me
and my story pretty much nothing gets resolved. At least
not like the way Mr. Fairfux says they should. I got my
job back as a security guard so I guess that part of the
story is resolved mostly but it took a while cause I had to
wait till the police investigation was done. I guess Truck
was doing lots of crimes and criminal things after he got
out so the police pretty much believed my side of the story
and I wasnt charged with nothing to do with Trucks death.
And Reverend Grainger didnt know about any of them
criminal things Truck did neither from what the police
said. Anyway I went back to watching people come and go on
a gray closed-circuit monitor in the security office of
Tower Plaza and I guess Rudy was happy to see me back
although we never did much together after that cause I
stopped going to Orions Belt My Ass after work and he
quit a while later anyway. Sometimes it was like I never
left Tower Plaza cause the people all looked pretty much

the same and the coffee tasted the same and the other guys
still talked about the same dumb things and sometimes I
thought of Jack stapling picture frames and his
bandaged hands and I wondered if I was like that now too.
Ray stopped in to see Jack now and then and I guess Jack
grew old real fast after mom died or maybe all the pills
he took finally caught up with him. I dont know. Then
after a year or so Ray quit the revival meetings and got a
job at a hamburger place. Not long after that he moved into
his own place and I guess I knew it was the right thing for
Ray to do but I still missed him being around the house
sometimes and in a way I guess he pretty much disappeared
from my life too. I guess it would be fair to say I was proud
of Ray mostly and I still felt like he was my brother. He
believed what he believed and no one could change it and
he was still happy he found the Lord or I guess the Lord
found him.

Like I said Truck died that night in the Kings Head Hotel.
And Rosie well she never woke up. I have to say it still
hurts real bad when I think about it. I guess the police
had to pry Rosie from my arms and I mean its probably
true although I dont remember it none. They took her to

St. Mikes and operated pretty much all night and I
remember it cause I sat and pretty much counted every
tile on the floor of the waiting room and the whole time I
was thinking about when we suckled in the theater during
the black and white war movie and I knew right then I
loved Rosie but I never said nothing. I guess I was hoping
for one more chance to say it this time but the chance
never came. So now Rosie is in a coma in the hospital and
the doctors dont know what will happen to her so I come in
to see her every day after my shift downtown and wait to
see if she wakes up or not so I can tell her I love her and I
was wrong to let her disappear when she did. I guess
sometimes I think about Sam too cause I never got the chance
to sit by her every day and just look at her and talk to her and
touch her hair cause she was just gone one day. She disappeared
from my life and left me with a sadness that ached all the
time and never went away mostly. Till I met Rosie I guess.
And as long as I can still come here and see Rosie I guess I
can still hope cause one day I might come here and shell
just sit up and say hi and well pretty much pick things up
where we left off. Mr. Fairfux says it makes a better
ending anyway when Rosie dont wake up and I just keep
waiting for something to happen that might never happen

and even if she does wake up he says well leave the ending like it is cause its more open and I guess thats a good thing when it comes to books. Mr. Fairfux read about my story in the newspaper about a month or so after that night at the Kings Head Hotel and he called to ask me if I would write a book about it and I said I guess I would. He said lots of people would be interested in the story of a man who one day finds himself lactating but Im not so sure about that myself. Anyway writing a book gives me something to do when I sit by Rosie every day and look at her and hope she wakes up. I guess the one thing that did get resolved was I stopped lactating after that night in the Kings Head Hotel. It stopped and it never started up again even when I think real hard about Rosie. So now its pretty much like it never happened and I guess Ill never know why it happened at all. Mr. Fairfux says it happened to other men before too but no one is really sure why. I mean I dont believe it was a gift from God like Reverend Grainger said but maybe it was a gift from somewhere anyway. At least for a little while.

So now I drive the Bel Air home from the hospital every night and I guess part of me hopes to see Phil out in the rose bushes but he never is. I was only gone a few months but the house dont seem like a home much no more so I park on the street like the way I always used to and I get out and walk up the new driveway to the house and I look at the rose bushes out front and they look like a big tangle of pink and yellow yarn or something. I take in the mail and open some windows and then I go into the kitchen and find a beer in the fridge and I crack the can and sit at the table alone. Sometimes when Im sitting there I see the dishes are done and I think maybe Phil came by when I was at the hospital cause I cant remember if I did them myself that morning or not. But anyway I still think maybe he came by and I take a drink of beer and think it would be okay if Phil came by again. And I think maybe if he did wed be okay again me and Phil. Then I finish my beer and I get another and I go downstairs and set the train to run for a while and when Im finally tired I go upstairs and drop onto the bed and I sleep like a stone until morning.

About the Author

Benjamin Salmon lives in Arkansas, where he teaches high school English. In his spare time he builds wooden stools. He doesn't collect model trains.

www.ingramcontent.com/pod-product-compliance
Lightning Source LLC
Chambersburg PA
CBHW061020120726
47910CB00006B/2036